FINAL QUESTIONS

Tiny Essays About Everything

FINAL QUESTIONS

Tiny Essays About Everything

Dennis J. Reader

www.sempervirensbooks.com

FOR FURTHER INFORMATION OR OTHER BOOKS

BY THE AUTHOR:

www.sempervirensbooks.com

sempervirensbooks@gmail.com

Editor's Contents

Author's Essays

One

Here we go. I wince a little, or a lot. I take a deep, deep breath, knowing that what follows will be dismissed as a fairy tale, although it isn't. Much more name it cold fact than fancy fiction. Much more consider it adventure of mind than mere adventure.

Yes, true, recently the love of my life left me, taking away my love of life itself. Yes, earlier yet I think I murdered my own mother So, yes, there I was, such as I was. Then something happened. On a very ordinary Tuesday morning at work a slim package addressed to me had arrived.

An innocent, undersized package had arrived, and I could never suspect that what I found inside would infect me like some stubborn disease—first as a farce, next as a narcotic, next as a vision, finally as reality. I already said this isn't a fairy tale.

And here we go.

That a manila envelope already waited on my desk was no surprise. Being an editor at a book publisher I still get plenty of these paper relics along with the digital copies of manuscripts. Indeed, with our particular subject focus we seem to be more old-fashioned than the giant commercial firms. A while ago I left one of those big famous "publishing houses" and at age thirty-one retreated to a sleepy niche publisher—my six colleagues here smilingly refer to us as a "publishing cabin"—where I hoped to better cubbyhole myself and mend a troubled heart. Of course I instead told everyone it was to avoid stress and reduce protracted arrhythmia episodes. I remember tapping my chest, ambiguously enough, to signify an internal medical problem, and they all understood because we specialize in the calm professional backwater of cookbooks and books for gardening hobbyists.

How to Dress Healthy Salads. The Illustrated Book of Waffles. Roses without End. Successful Steps to Better Mulch. Inside the envelope mailer on my desk should have been a manuscript with a tediously predictable title like these.

No, no, no.

FINAL QUESTIONS the title page read. *Tiny Essays.*

Okay. What was up here exactly? Page One, Essay #1, was up exactly.

Essay #1

Explaining Humanity in 2⅔ Words

Stars can't cry.

[Explication: A supernova doesn't give a shit about its end.
But even a flatworm tries to stay alive.]

Well, hard to ignore, when a crude profanity greets you, glaring there amid a blunderbuss blast of empty paper space. Maybe I was more puzzled than thrown back. Any prankster, or any buffoon, can submit a manuscript to us. No law against it.

Eventually I went digging for the author's cover letter where I hoped to find . . . actually, what could I hope to find? Whatever, I didn't.

The author, one "B. Bartleby," Ph.D., true to the tiny essays, kept any background information brief. He or she (impossible to know with that single initial) was "fiftyish," had toiled for fourteen years at the federal patent office in a major city, scrutinizing the authenticity of thousands of technical applications—from the brilliant to the absurd, the "absurd" occasionally being the most "brilliant." After that fourteenth year Dr. Bartleby up and quit this position, moving to a southern countryside where he or she bought thirty acres of land, intending to farm pomegranates and "spend a minimum of six hours daily t-h-i-n-k-i-n-g." Not a word was mentioned about the essays themselves or their purpose or any of the normal blather that editors find in introductory letters from authors.

Other than the unlikely pomegranate reference, I spotted no imaginable connection between these essays and me.

At first, like any person of cautious reason, I reviewed the evidence. I double-checked. I confirmed: thirty essays in the entirety. thirty pages in the entirety. Using my finger and thumb I touched, turned, and counted each page. No doubt about it, only thirty pages in the aggregate, with each separate page a home for its own separate tiny essay, the "tiny" part being a massive exaggeration. Subsequently, again like any person of reason, I expected to return the manuscript immediately, since my company could never publish such a whatever-it-is thing, or as if any publisher anywhere would.

The reasonable never happened.

I didn't return Dr. Bartleby's manuscript.

What did I do? I began a lengthy lying performance of playing a potential editor. I confess to this. It just started, for some purpose or other, or for no purpose. I just started somehow. One day I began sending messages. And he or she never failed to reply promptly.

----

*As you claim, as the experienced editor you are, perhaps my book would attract a larger readership if its title were changed to **Final Answers**. But I wonder.*

*Answers tend to scare me off. Answers can function too often as a poison, sterilizing the soil, not letting new ideas or new questions sprout and grow. Did you yourself not edit a book titled **The Royal Legacy of Soil Amendment**?*

*And personally, since you ask, my intention is not "to seek final truths." In undramatic fact, all I expect of myself is to **think** honestly, to the degree that I can manage. If along the way I seem, or am, a fool, allow me to act as a bold fool rather than a timid one. I would feel much disappointment if I ended a lazy life without asking a few questions—those Final Questions. Absolutely, my motives are primarily selfish. I demand my right to follow simple curiosity. I demand my turn and my right to speak aloud. I demand my right to be wrong.*

Essay #2

A Description of Mortality for You

[Explication: This page intentionally left blank.]

Dear Dr. Bartleby:

Again, as an editor, I have to complain that you, Dr. Bartleby, fail to throw out any life preservers to your readers, and instead let them bob alone there in the vast sea of philosophy with only a few scattered words to keep them afloat. Or no words at all! It's like dumping a beginning swimmer in the middle of the Pacific Ocean with the advice, "Head for shore. Try to find an island."

Dr. Bartleby, you might realize how challenging it is to solve even the flimsiest of those Big Problems we may face? Consider the difficulty of preparing, merely, a proper Christmas roast, a subject I professionally know something about. First comes a decision about a suitable meat, having to decide between, as a minimum, beef or pork or lamb or chicken or turkey or duck. Which best pleases your guests? Can you be certain? Will the meat be fresh or frozen? How many days before Christmas should you buy the meat, and heaven forbid, could it suddenly not be available, all sold out to more aggressive shoppers? Exactly that tragedy happened two years ago at Flannery's Market, and three years ago at The Meat Depot. And what type of juice to baste the roast with: honey soy? wine marinade? butter gravy? bacon drippings? Add cloves? Add garlic? And what china platter should we place the roast on, the green or the orange? Don't forget the apple sauce. Or maybe use cranberry sauce. And will the one important guest you truly wish to be sitting at the dining table, with smiling brown eyes on the other side of four flickering holiday-red candles, show up to join you?

So very, very much can go wrong in this world, Dr. Bartleby, with many, many lurking pitfalls. We have no control, I feel. Each day teaches me lessons about my own helplessness.

Your attention please. Our planet Earth rotates at 1,000 miles per hour. Or make it 900 MPH at the 35th parallel, where currently I happen to stand. **Whizzzz!**

Hold on tight and we continue. The blue marble called Earth, besides rotating, also revolves at 67,000 MPH along a 600-million-mile path around our fireball sun, while the sun flies through our Milky Way galaxy, towing along the earth. Our Milky Way wheels, at 500,000 MPH, along a rotation that takes a quarter of a billion years to complete, carrying with it our sun. Our galaxy is flung through space at 1,300,000 MPH by our Local Group of galaxies, this group pulled by larger collections of groups, these groups by forces ancient and new, gigantic energies both known and unknown.

I walk. I walk down a hallway to a kitchen to make a bowl of pomegranate soup, an acquired taste. My question is: How fast, really, all velocities considered, am I moving?

Answer: It depends on how hungry I am.

That earth, that sun, the galaxies, the cosmos, must march their speedy way to the set beat of programmatic fate. I may choose to move my sluggish feet a little faster or a little slower, adding to or subtracting from that combined fate.

And here comes the shocker. I may choose not to move my feet at all. I may even choose to stand and stand, without any bowls of soup, until I starve and die, thereby creating my own separate fate. In this sense the mechanical cosmos is itsy-bitsy and I am immense. In this sense the cosmos is helpless and I am omnipotent.

Essay #3

Free Will

The proper spelling is freed will.

[Explication: Not the platitude "mind over matter,"
but "minds matter."]

Dear Dr. Bartleby:

Now what can I do? In recent months I'd started more and more depending on some principle of Inevitability to interpret my life, which Dr. Bartleby wants to take away from me, if I halfway understand it.

Except should I give up such a placating idea? And how can anyone ever prove, for certain, that we're not an invisible thread in a huge web of preordained events, programmed within us and outside us, and although we believe in knowing what the heck is going on, in truth we have no choice or chance to alter the outcome of a single event. We live a deception of motives.

For instance. For instance a young woman and young man meet one day at a supermarket, bumping into each other in the fresh produce section, at the asparagus bin, the asparagus on sale for $1.99 a bundle. His elbow jarred, he drops a bundle of this asparagus, and she retrieves it for him. He wears a silver hoodie with a soaring eagle's dark silhouette printed on the broad front. She wears her aquamarine sweater which brings out the highlights of her shampooed hair. Someone's brown eyes smile. The two talk, they joke, they flirt, and begin to date/date/date. Their favorite food is the same, spaghetti. Their favorite music is the same, 1940s swing. Their favorite pastime is the same, snuggling. They kiss madly. They declare love madly. At their wedding, friends call them "the happiest-looking couple this side of a gushy Hollywood romance movie." In their first apartment home the young man and the young woman continue to snuggle, to kiss, declare love, and eat spaghetti. Then about five years and three months later, on an early evening at about six o'clock, one of the two comes home and tells the other, "We need a divorce."

Please, how to understand this as anyone's preventable "choice"? Impossible. It had to be stacked in the cosmic cards. It had to be waiting to happen, like night always follows a sunset. The young woman and the young man bear no fault, no more than being responsible for arriving at the asparagus bin together at the exact same moment.

Dr. Bartleby will probably do a head-shake and comment, "Someone apparently did choose. Suck it up, buttercup."

No buttercups. But dear, dear me—what hard choices there are to make about the subject of choice, including choosing if there is any choice. You have to choose not to choose? Wait. Did I just prove the validity of "free will" choice? No?

Dear, dear, what then should a child decide to believe, especially because deciding might not be a real decision in the first place, or in the last place. This topic of free will has put Thinkers into a tizzy since before the ancient Greeks. Volition is such a heavy burden to carry. Better, instead of choices, to pass the load on to a Guiding Hand? To Spirits possibly? Deities? Providence? Karma? Nature-Nurture? Neurons? Dear, dear.

Unfortunately nagging problems do arise in life without admitting to at least a smidgen of free will (this illogical notion of a fractional free will we offer gratis to any stand-up comic). With no personal volition in our actions, Evil and Sin quickly lose sense, as do Praise and Honor. Who cares a fig or a pomegranate about your young man and young woman from the asparagus bin, with their grand love, if the two of them could never have avoided their love and marriage from the start. Romance would always be a big yawn. Our very own Calvinist pilgrims trapped themselves inside a similar theological box of predestination, did they not? If Original Sin by mankind had cast us all into inevitable damnation—omitting a handful rescued to demonstrate the Guiding Hand's power of mercy—then Good Deeds would never earn a ticket into salvation, although acting out these Good Deeds might impress your neighbors into believing you could be a lucky winner. No wonder that nowadays some philosophers try out theories of "levels" of free will, but these efforts dissipate into a verbal fog denser than hearing physicists decode quantum magic.

*My skepticism about some brand of predestination does not discount any type of **influence** in human life, whether probability percentages, biology, propensities, or even happenstance. There existed **reasons** why the young woman and young man arrived at the asparagus bin together. They both had time available to grocery shop, at least. They both must have enjoyed eating asparagus, at least. One of them must have had the genetic heritage to form attractive brown eyes, at least. Yet those reasons—locked into irreversible position only by rewinding the interlinked chronology of events—will not mean the young man and young woman had been forced to meet for their asparagus, nor forced to feel love.*

*The determinists would disagree. Such pure theorists would seize on every action of the young woman and young man, every probability and improbability in their lives, dismiss them as fictional categories, and handily loop each triggered step backward, connected to an endless external circle of causation. A loop is a loop is a **reductio ad absurdum** loop.*

And the latest adventure into deterministic behavior is studied by neuroscientists in laboratories, who seek the locus for *every human act, namely its instigation by a chemical dousing and electrical crackling in the brain, an interior switching sequence that makes our decisions for us. The neurologist-philosopher applies sensors to a cerebrum, has the subject, for example, drink a tumbler of whiskey, observes the synapses in the brain trigger on-and-off, and records the subject's behavior. Then, by golly, without any liquor, the same switches can be flipped in the same order and the subject still acts a little drunk! What might be extrapolated from these experiments, you wonder. Can we propose, perhaps, that we could today replicate Shakespeare in 1605, who while periodically drinking the right amount of ale, not getting tipsy, not exactly sober either, and we can make his same 1,304,403 necessary decisions—without willing them—to write **King Lear**?*

Enough of my being smarty-assed about it. All closed mechanisms, simple or complex, have a vital delimiting brake built into them. If the brain were a gun, and its neural network and chemistry the spark and powder, when ignited what fires out is a bullet of energy—but not a "thought," that separate item with its own special existence. Here certainly is the classic case of the whole being greater than the sum of its parts.

While speaking of "thoughts," why not conclude with one, and ponder whether our neuroscientist comrades are conducting their research without any independent control over their minds to determine that they do not control their minds.

Dear Dr. B:

I can tell that the whole argument about "thought" and the independence of it, and control over it, gets under your skin. Believe me. I personally am proof of the power of uncontrollable thoughts, because they get under my whole spirit, not only under my skin. By my spirit I probably mean my sanity. Am I permitted to mention "my sanity"? Well, only in poor taste, when writing to an outsider and a prospective client, and excuse me for that, my dear Dr B.

But these thoughts, or memory pictures mainly, keep building an indestructible world inside, while my mind seems to be running out of room to hold any more of the debris. Pictures, pictures, pictures, pictures. At what point will my inside world outweigh the world outside? Sounds risky.

Essay #4

Remembering Memory

Nothing kills faster than forgetting kills.

[Explication: Did Grandpa ever smile at me?]

Two

Eventually I had to leave Dr. Bartleby's manuscript at home, because at the office I constantly caught myself with it at my desk, rocked back in my chair, reading a page or two, staring into ceiling space, re-reading another page or two. My colleagues had noticed. "What you working on there?" they asked. I said, "Fruit. Plums, apricots, pomegranates." They said, "Must be a good read." I lied, "Not really."

My daydreaming only continued and, sans manuscript, followed me back to work again. Dr. Bartleby's Essay #4 nagged at me for a week. I attempted to retrieve my memories of my own grandfather, who died when I was three or four. Fuzzy visions formed of my sitting on his lap with him smelling slightly of roasted coffee . . . or roasted peanuts. And I could almost hear sounds of us talking, my squeaky child's voice patching together clumsy sentences. But these wishful illusions evaporated. I didn't remember my grandfather. Those photographs of him in our family album had no more life to them, for me, than a photograph of Abraham Lincoln. My grandfather was gone, reduced to a schematic placeholder branch on a family tree, without any connection inside anybody's breathing flesh-and-touch world.

Dr. Bartleby must be correct. After a couple of generations—past your great-grandkids or so—you're erased from the surface of the living earth, when the last memory of the last person is scrubbed clean. Even if tales about grandfathers continue to be told—folktales—no listener will smell the roasted coffee or feel the warm hand.

Dear Dr. B:

Tell me, could we run the effects of this memory business backward, do you suppose? My question is, can you eliminate a memory before its time, particularly before it wants to leave, or before you have to die to get rid of it? To take Essay #4 figuratively, or do I mean literally, how would one person go about killing off another person, a dangerous person, who kept burrowing into your mind, making you sick?

The potency of memory—a corollary to the potency of thought—is as real as dropping a brick on your bare foot. People have been known to destroy themselves to destroy their memories. Psychiatrists identify these suicidal thoughts as a disease.

Better, why not admit the importance of memory, its value, and ultimately, its necessity. Memory is our ladder of experience and learning. Memory is our antidote to the forward arrow of time. Memory allows us to make ourselves human. It might even be said that excessive memory (ratcheted up to the point of neurosis) creates our greatest art, or our attempt to encapsulate memory and become immortal.

*Yet memories, the rascals, resist segregating themselves into good apples and bad apples. Memories have happened, they just **are**, and they form us into ourselves. People, to be complete, seem to need all the apples, including the sour one, including the proverbial rotten one, including the weird pomegranate apple (wink, wink).*

If we should not, or cannot, destroy an unhappy memory, try greeting it with a polite nod of recognition as we scoot by, on our way to other more pleasant activities, like keeping the happier memories healthy and thriving, along with any grandfathers.

Why does giving good advice always leave behind an uncomfortable overload of sugary aftertaste? Presently it feels like I need to brush my teeth.

Essay #5

Is Time Real?

Please hold your breath for 23 minutes.

[Explication: Unfortunately some evidence can only
be confirmed by its elimination.]

Dear Dr. B:

Yesterday I tried joking with Herbert, my co-editor for the book *Secrets to a Successful Brunch*, by using Essay #5 on him, saying "Herbie, I read about a major breakthrough discovery, in an experiment at Princeton, that *finally* proves the reality of time. And guess what. We can duplicate the proof right here in our office, right now." Herbert ranks as our best detail worker, superb at reviewing book galleys for typos. He asked me, "Us? Without a lab or lasers?" "Without lasers. Just take off your wristwatch in order to follow the time count better." "Got it off." "Next keep your eye on the watch and hold your breath for twenty-three minutes." "Got it. Twenty-three seconds." "No," I told him, "twenty-three minutes." "I can't hold my breath for twenty-three minutes." "Twenty-two minutes then." "I can't hold my breath for twenty-two minutes either." "I'll tape up your mouth and nose. We have plenty of binder tape there in the patch drawer." "Holy Toledo, I'd be dead." "Herbie, think about it, how we get to demonstrate that time is an actual thing, same as the big brains at Princeton did." Herbert put back on his wristwatch, went to his desk, sat, sat some more, and whispered quietly as a mouse in a church, down toward his desktop, "I don't follow any of this."

I was careful, Dr. B, never to smirk at my own joke or at Herbert, because I like him. But I'd hoped Herbert might tease me back with something like, "And I don't have TIME for nonsense." No such luck.

Of all the top ten tunes ever sung, "What Funny Business Is Time?" ranks up there with the greatest hits, alongside "Am I Actually Me?" and "Are Humans the Smartest Things Anywhere?' and "Where Did All Stuff Come from in the First Place?" or that mega-blockbuster, "Where Do I Arrive When I Leave to Die?"

Time's irresistible melody means many singers have recorded their own versions of it. Check the Internet to hear a slew of amateurs belting out—often from a home couch holding a solo guitar—the most popular interpretation of Time, the folk version, re-titled "My Lifetime." I enjoy this version myself, because I can wrap Time around my daily autobiography, beginning with . . . well, with my birth, and moving forward guided by familiar calendars and clocks. Surprisingly, I can play with Time, bending the notes to suit my mood, or by upping the tempo to express excitement and slowing it down for regret or anticipation. And then there is memory—our Time companion from Essay #4—which allows us to repeat the first stanzas of the song after already performing them.

To continue with my music analogy (advise me if music and time are more siblings than an analogy) we can move from foot-tapping folk tune to Time symphony, a majestic composition that has no start and no conclusion. All physical events did not/ will not occur together at a single, isolated, timeless Once. Just as all matter does not simultaneously occupy the same restricted non-space, all events do not occupy the same non-moment. Thus process = time. Eternal time is why using the term "singularity" in cosmology is a misnomer.

*So time is process or sequence—speed it up, squeeze it, reverse it—whatever the theorists choose to quantify. Even a pause is a rhythmic measure inside symphonic Time. And because time is a process or sequence, and not a **thing**, it can never be destroyed or be absent. Time is forever present, waiting to happen with you.*

Time has no genesis because time must always be. Such a concept should not be impossible for us to conceive. As with infinity, there always exists the "before" to add before any Before—and this is not clever wordplay. For time is also not a *vacuous **potential** that has meaning or existence only when we, or any other hard matter, interact with it, inventing it. Instead we are the potential that interacts with time.*

Accepting eternal Time provides a partial comfort to nervous human minds. Eternity is a priceless pretty package all by itself. However our lifetime Time is not eternal, and awareness of that condition is a familiar testimony to—and curse of—human perception. Our short period of personal consciousness reaches an end, our legal presence within the sequence finishes, although other less charming subsets of ourselves, at the molecular and atomic levels, continue to join the process called Time.

Best not to bother Herbie with these ideas.

Essay #6

How to Measure Infinity

Just keep counting until the end.

[Explication: Nope, you're not there yet.]

Dr. B:

Dr. B, Dr. B, to keep on and on daydreaming, eyes open, with this *Final Questions* manuscript on my mind, is understandable, given the lure of its questions. But night dreams, eyes shut, take me into deeper escapes, apparently without my wanting the journey to happen, unless it *is* my want. I wonder if you, Dr. B, ever use night dreams. Or do daydreams suffice.

The hour must be late since I crawled into bed long ago. My room is colored Total Black or my eyes see black. This must be sleep. Despite the blackness my dream is bright, so white and bright it demands to act like a revelation. Illuminated by this whiteness—unfolding the way a morning glory opens its petals to the sunrise—are the stupendous promises of your infinity with its endless Time. Purely put, infinity promises all promises, and fulfills each one with a guarantee.

Hard to pick where to start with the wonder of these perfect promises. Infinity requires that every allowable combination of future possibilities will come to pass. Infinity requires that every occurrence from the past will repeat itself to become part of that same future. Am I thinking straight, Dr. B? Or dreaming straight?

—Each and every atom will resume the precise location it once held.

—Each raindrop will therefore fall in concert on the same blade of grass.

—Every gust of wind will therefore blow in the same direction under the same clouds.

—The identical birds will therefore sail in these identical winds.

—The same trees will therefore be cut into the same boards to build the same houses.

—The same asparagus plants will therefore be harvested from the same farmer's field and delivered to the same asparagus bin to be sold at the same grocery store.

—The same young woman and young man will therefore . . .

Maybe this is a truth that only a dream can tell. Maybe this is only a dream. But I do sleep a nudge better.

I enjoyed your enthusiasm—which rang out as poetic even—a positive quality too scarce in your earlier messages. Enthusiasm is infectious, and I caught myself sneezing recently. Thank you.

For you, infinity provides comforting thoughts, you explain, because it dictates that whatever is lost must inevitably return. I respect your intellectual grasp of the infinite. Nevertheless, from your occupation you also understand the wisdom of editing a massive 1,000-page manuscript. And no book has more pages than infinity does.

Infinity, it turns out, is a tricky affair, tricky enough to consider that your young man and young woman will have met again at the asparagus bin already, innumerable times already, eaten their spaghetti together again, had their sad six o'clock evening meal again, gotten divorced again and again. Accordingly some editorial work is in order. Among all the infinite repeat meetings of the young woman and young man, pick out a subtle variation, one where the two are only "almost" the same young man and young woman. Now they could be shopping for broccoli instead of asparagus. Now their favorite food could be melted cheese sandwiches. Now switch one of them from brown eyes to blue. Now make one of them less lonely, the other less frightened. These small editorial alterations might add up to seventy years of successful marriage.

Another cautionary warning. Never forget, the journey through Forever means a trip without a final destination. Patience is an incomplete tool for the infinite. Since infinity refuses to reach a finish, the young woman and young man may endlessly be held inside a matching state of waiting, where their happy marriage never bothers to arrive, if you follow my mad logic. Then again, they might get lucky, very lucky, and jostle into themselves again at a food store sometime during infinity's flow.

*But, but, but. If the young man and young woman should connect again, they would say "Hello," **but** not "Hello again." They would believe themselves strangers. There could be no recollection of past asparagus bins, or soaring eagles, or soaring hearts, because their cognitive lives are new, having started from birth at point zero. "Nothing kills faster than forgetting kills."*

Dr. B:

Shucks, Dr. B, let's wish the young woman and young man their stroke of gigantic good luck. We'll cross our fingers that the two come together again Sooner rather than Later (later, as in the other side of Never). And the two will turn up as the necessary corrected combination of themselves, like the jackpot tumblers in a Las Vegas slot machine. Stubbornly, I won't let you be a complete spoilsport, Dr. B, and the brown eyes must stay unchanged. Flip the asparagus to string beans, but brown eyes will always be brown eyes. I never cheat when I edit. In my books about roses, a rose is always named a rose, despite what W. Shakespeare said.

As least you avoided the false solution of pointing out to me that the young man and woman could already have had their happy marriage, at some past point in infinity's history, and the current two of them simply were clueless about it and their happiness. I appreciate not being offered the cold comfort of the theoretical.

Abstractions upon abstractions. They don't warm the bed beside you at night.

How about another approach for the young couple.

Rather than playing games of chance, rather than depending on future events, instead utilize what you remember as real. Our old friend memory is not an invalid substance, not a random puff of cerebral activity. Memories are not fiction unless we falsely manipulate them. What happened in the past between the young man and young woman is immutable, safe from any dishonest reinterpretation, or cynical editing, to adopt your apt verb.

Yesterdays can never be denied, never have a limit, never a shelf life, and yesterdays are as authentic as any today. A true "I love you" spoken in the past is as legitimate as an "I love you" pledged today—and tomorrow. More importantly for brown eyes everywhere, a true "I love you" given five years and three months ago is equally genuine as—and conceivably more valuable than—an "I don't love you" given five years and two months ago.

No thief steals a yesterday. That would be against an inviolate law.

Three

This *Final Questions* book or whatever. This Dr. B. Bartleby person or whoever. There came a morning (only this morning it always seems) when early out of bed I looked into the mirror and asked myself, with a shiver at my bare shoulders:

Have I somehow lost the solid handle of sanity? Have I gone adrift inside a mushy cloud of foolishness?

Or has fate put a skinny manuscript on my desk to hold steady these same shaking shoulders? Instead of foolishness, could I be the luckiest fool in the world?

The period of snickering about the essays had quickly passed. The period of attempting to ignore them had come and gone. The period of denial had ended. The period of hoping to exhaust them had failed. The battle to resist my increasing dependency was over.

I needed to read those crazy microscopic essays.

And I needed the faithful Dr. B.

At the editorial offices I studied Franklin McDermott, our chief publisher, as he sat in a far corner, at a commanding desk. With his big bald spot and a trim compensating goatee and a frequent grin, he's a decent fellow, a dedicated worker, accommodating to others, gentle almost. Could Franklin ever be convinced to publish *Final Questions*?

Can we empty all the oceans today? Heaven save me.

Essay #7

When Did Everything All Begin?

It never did.

[Explication: To begin requires an existing end: to end requires a previous beginning. Eternity is another word for existence.]

Essay #8

How Did Everything Not Begin Forever?

I need you so much, my darling, I couldn't
live without you.

[Explication: "To be, or not to be, that is the question"
is not a question.]

Essay #9

Why Did Everything Never Not Finish?

Why not.

[Explication: Eternity forgets to have motives.]

Dr. B:

"Which came first, the chicken or the egg?" is the ancient riddle that sideways fits essays #7-#8-#9 while also reminding me how my own father distracted me with this question one summer afternoon when he was teaching me to ride a bike, and I fell, tearing my clothes, both of us examining my skinned knees. "The chicken needs an egg to make the chicken. The egg needs a chicken to make the egg. You see the problem. Forget about the knees for a minute, and tell me, which came first. Forget those knees. Look up, tell me." He had an engaging smile, my father, a type of boyish impulsive smile that anybody had to believe. His name was Stewart. Most likely I cried a little on that summer day, or whimpered bravely, I hope. We always want to impress our fathers.

Hey, what's this sentimental tug pulling me back to my personal family history? I'll resist it.

Your essays, Dr. B, state (as I become more and more accustomed to the stingy sentences) there was no chicken first and no egg first, but that both of them, or what they developed in tandem to become, always existed. Just as time's process can have no possible beginning, all our Chicken Matter of existence can have no start, because from what absence of matter could matter ever start. Chickens since Forever is a humongous pill for us mortal humans to swallow, but I see your point.

My father never gave me his solution to the chicken riddle, the idea being there is no answer, or better not be any answer, because in his case that would spoil the fun. He liked joking, my father, to go along with his smile. In contrast my mother might have said, "My little sweetheart, listen, God made the chicken first with the egg already inside, don't you suppose?" But would she have had her tongue in her cheek? Impossible to guess with my mother. Her humor came without the helpful hint of a smile, that deadpan face making the joke funnier, she assumed. For me, watching my parents meant watching a ping-pong match between personalities, my dad with his transparent policy of smiles and chuckles, my mom with her door kept tight shut, not allowing even a glimmer of a twinkle to escape from those hazel eyes. It spun a kid's head dizzy sometimes, stuck there in the middle of those two people.

Listen to me jaw on and on. Apparently I *won't* resist rambling away about myself, after all. Will you indulge me, Dr. B, or please scold me if I veer too far from your manuscript, although your essays must be triggering this fall into my private story. Still, I hope never to blame you for my neglect of any editorial duties.

I do want you to understand, Dr. B, my father and mother formed a successful link-up for one another, successful in that they would have, should have, been happily married until the ends of a long natural life. Looking back (memories again) I recognize a devotion between my parents, no matter how badly everything ended, and the ending was awful. And I try to accept, if I can accept it, that the bad ending alone proved the devotion.

Even as a youngster I noticed the signs of their affection. In my opinion, those hundreds of small signals represent more love than an occasional big flashy declaration. I wanted for myself whatever I saw, when I grew up. I wanted those mini-moments together with somebody. Considered from an odd peculiar angle, later in my life I felt jealous of my parents, because they had put together a relationship that held tight, unlike many other couples, such as that pair who only ate spaghetti together for a short while.

My father had several tours of duty with the U.S. Marines, off in one of those sort-of-war wars we read about in the newspapers and history books. He came back a bit roughed up around the edges but steadied down enough to enroll in college, which he finished right on schedule in four years with a degree in geology. Why geology? Nobody explained that for me, including my father, and he spent his whole career as an administrator for a major power utility company. A large man, with hands the size of pie plates, when he dressed in a suit and tie it looked all wrong to me, and maybe to him. Once when quite young I asked, "Do you climb those telephone poles like the guys with spikes on their boots?" He smiled his smile, saying, "Only if you get yourself stuck up there trying to rescue your dumb kitten."

My father never spoke much about his Marine days, although he had one military habit that never went away and never, literally, left our house. I refer to a Beretta M9 pistol, a 9mm exact twin to his service handgun. Ignoring my mother's protests he would lecture me, holding the weapon, not smiling for once, "I'll protect, it'll protect, Mommy and you, always. Nobody will ever hurt you two." His voice sent a chill down my childhood backbone. I still feel that coldness today.

We moved three times while I was younger and after each move my father made clear I knew without any hesitation where the Beretta was hidden. The older I got the more details I had to learn about a Beretta M9, the way other kids take after-school math lessons. Semi-automatic. 15-round magazine. Effective range (55 yards). Even its muzzle velocity (1250 ft/s). On my twelfth birthday my father showed me how to dry-fire the gun plus how to load and insert the magazine. On my thirteenth birthday I had to practice finding and loading the Beretta in the dark. "I could be away on one of my business trips," explained my father. "We can't imagine in this world what turns up next." For my sixteenth birthday we were scheduled for my first trip to a practice range, an actual firing range, which never quite came to pass.

Enough of this. Anyhow, I wish my father were around to read your essays, Dr. B, especially numbers #7-#8-#9. His mind, the mind that for whatever reason chose to study geology, would have appreciated wondering where all those rocks and dirt and eggs came from in the "first" place. I believe I just saw him smile.

I sense, more than sense, the emotional heft of a story behind your stories, growing in size by consuming its own previous silence. You should be writing books instead of editing them?

Be advised! I expect to hear your personal story, wish to hear it, require it, because this puts up a human sounding board for my manuscript. Please do not disappoint me by retreating now. After all, we seek to tie together the airy contemplation of the essays with our bone-and-blood world, particularly as we confront the most heavyweight of Final Questions. Some Thinkers judge these current topics as the fattest of the heavyweights:

> *—The origin of Origin.*

> *—The creation of the Creator.*

> *—The beginning of Beginning.*

> *—The start of Start.*

> *—The wait before the Arrival.*

> *—The absence before the Presence.*

> *—The nothing before the Something.*

We probe the farthermost into the skies above us and into our minds inside us to understand what seems unfathomable. Would it be strange if these vastly mysterious unknowns on our list had the briefest of conclusions? What if every search, every question above, depended on a word that is not a functioning word? What if each question above depends on a word that cannot even say its own name?

Creatio ex nihilo, *the classical Latin expression for "creation out of nothing," is a self-canceling metaphysical* *vapor, as likewise is its traditional opponent **Ex nihilo nihil fit**, "nothing comes from nothing." Both sides of this venerable argument use the word that cannot say its name: **nothing**.*

Shall we try speaking about the unspeakable? Well, then. "No-thing" is not a "thing" and therefore can never be described and thereby never discussed, because it never exists. "Nothingness" presents us with a condition of impossibility that exceeds semantics, or ultimately, conception itself. And what is impossible leaves only the possible, or existence.

*Before we trample roughshod over our daily lives, we should remember that our handy language serves our basic needs well, including the word **nothing**. And the cipher **zero** provides a sensible and required placeholder purpose in mathematical calculations. When a student tells us, "I learned **nothing** from today's lesson," we interpret that to mean he or she did indeed learn **something**: "I learned that I did not learn." These secondary applications of "nothingness" should not be mistaken for the word that cannot define itself.*

When we begin considering all these blurry questions, such as chickens and eggs, origins of matter, space and time, our language readily breaks down into verbs without action, pronouns without antecedents, nouns without substance. We might ask, "Can we think without language, and if our language is unreliable, what can we comprehend for a certainty?" Some linguists claim our language map of the world is our only knowable reality. I agree that language and mathematics, and science overall, are human systems of labels, useful and probably indispensable systems intending to describe, or "humanize," for us a comprehended reality. Language, and other impressive cerebral maps, are themselves powerful to the degree that they can construct their separate inner reality, a reality actually capable of cause and effect. But such ad hoc systems, profound in whatever ways, always reduce back inside the boundaries of labels.

*Like it or not (and we might not), there must be a reality beyond our language and thus beyond us. We should modestly consider that we **Homo sapiens** only recently arrived into this outer reality, and that our language, with our various other symbols, came more recently yet.*

I just hurried back after a short break outside in my pomegranate orchard. The fresh air jolts the mind awake after slogging through these philosophical swamps. But I intend not to leave you, and me, stranded in the middle of unclean water for long, and we should carry on toward the other shore. (Do editors despise labored metaphors?)

While out under my pomegranates I thought about your description of your father, which led me to my father, a man who had a notable smile in his own right. Once when I had turned old enough to read some philosophy, or dabble in it, I asked my father a question about epistemology—the study of whether we can positively know what we believe we know—and he answered, "Epistemology? Sounds like something you should do into a toilet." My father, I might mention, was a professor of Philosophy, and taught that subject his whole short life. Agreed—the pomegranate never falls far from its father's tree, does it not? To reciprocate your previous reminiscences about your own father, and to prompt more of them, I will pass on another story about mine. His specialty field in philosophy was Ethics. My father typically opened the first day of his classes by writing on the chalkboard the old condemnation: "Those who **can***, do it, those who* **can't***, teach it." After a theatrical pause he would write down a second sentence: "Guess why I'm teaching you ethics this semester!" According to my father, the students hardly ever laughed.*

Like you, when as a young person and trying to keep up with my father, I first came across the mind-twister of the Chicken or Egg dilemma, only in my case it was reading in a philosophy book about the history of the famous paradoxical statement "This sentence is a lie." This tidbit of self-referential confusion has generated over three millennia of argumentative ink from scholars. And now, between us, today, I want to make certain that our (impossible) discussion of the word "nothingness" is not dismissed as only another musical chairs game of logic or language, done mainly for academic sport.

"This sentence is a lie."

Even my youthful mind had quickly spotted the paradox planted in the circular deduction that if the sentence is a lie, then the sentence instead must be true, then if a truth, then indeed it must be a lie, then truth, then lie, then truth—around and around the dog chases its tail. Supposedly we could at least calm the dog by declaring: "This sentence is true." Truth is good, but what is true about the sentence (referral component as yet not specified)? "This sentence is a lie." A lie is bad, but what about the sentence is it lying about (referral component not yet specified)? Until the underlying reference is quantified for us the sentences hold the potential to be either truth or lie, or both simultaneously, or ambivalent. A meaningful judgment requires a meaningful evaluation requires a meaningful sentence.

More to our point, what happens when in place of the initial statement we write:

"This sentence is nothing."

Can we duplicate any similar paradox here, and rescue the logic and the dog? Can we claim that a not-a-thing is after all a thing, thereby making the sentence false? Or claim that a nothing is no different from a something is no different from a nothing is no different from a something? But this circle is a cycle of contradiction, not a paradox.

There is no dog to save. The word that cannot say its name—because its experience and concept do not exist—can function in a sentence only for alternate purposes. "This sentence is nothing" equals:

"Disregard this sentence."

There is no nothingness. And with that remark I create once again another of those sentences where a verb and a noun vanish beyond language. Unlike the apparent paradox "This sentence is a lie," my sentence with "nothingness" does not permit so much as an editorial sidebar fistfight over such classifications as what Truth and Lie might precisely mean. Losing these options of disputation would have disappointed my professorial father thoroughly, and reduced the number of his Ethics classes to teach.

Of course we should not forget your mother's tease (her voluble non-smile) about the Chicken and the Egg, and how they might have arrived together, the finished product of an initial First Creator. But then what of the creation of the First Creator? What then stood before this "first"? Nothing came before? The word that cannot say its name? If the First Creator is eternal, there can be no "first," and eternity itself is creation itself.

*Even we transitory beings can accept ideas of eternity or infinity, without cloaking them in human dimensions by naming them First Enablers or Guiding Hands. Already we conceive and construct absolutes, understanding fully the reality of always having One more than More, One less than Less. And we fearful beings can accept, should accept, that although we do comprehend these absolutes, do play a part in them, in the end our personal selves are not eternal. Spare the obfuscation of pleading **Why**, as if we humans deserve a special dispensation, a method of escape, an immortality of our very own. The answer to any question **Why** is not found up in the sky. The question **Why** is a human invention, and perhaps both the flower, and the thorn, of our intelligence.*

Of the two options for origin of matter and existence—whether existence always was, or if existence spontaneously appeared from non-existence—only the former is possible by logic or definition, despite not fitting inside our personal mortal context. Scientists might well attempt to big bang a First Cause out of "nothingness" or seek to speed and smash a something out of "nothing." Regardless of what impressive system of symbols we construct, whether linguistic or mathematical, regardless of what quantum slingshot we assemble, we will never describe or discover what never exists. Eventually, the last defender of First Cause creation retreats to a FAITH belief for support. But depending on faith, at the core, underneath, subtracts itself down to one of two complaints: "I can't imagine any other answer" or "I don't want any other answer."

Existence is already the answer. Existence always speaks its name, listened to or not.

Essay #10

What Do You Make When You Think?

You.

[Explication: When you break your heart, it's not
the one that beats blood.]

Essay #11

How Do I Love Thee?
Let Me Count the Way

Sum to me your mind, for I want a number
that high.

[Explication: Our kiss pleasures me most when
your lips whisper words.]

Essay #12

Translate the Latin *Fiat Lux* into English

And then man invented the light switch.

[Explication: The brightest shine known in the universe is discovered in faces.]

Dear Dr. B:

After spending "time" (a term awkward for me to use lately) digesting the complexities of your commentary on existence/eternity, I almost granted myself a day away from your manuscript. But then came the essays where the words "heart" and "love" and "kiss" jumped out at me. So onward I read. What a greedy victim I am for romance. What's more, your *Fiat Lux* title also hooked my interest because my mother could moderately read Latin, I found out. Back in college, where she met my father, her subject major had been Languages. In part I blame her for this eyesight-crippling job I have today.

My father Stewart classified his wife as, quote, a prime example of Brains and Beauty, unquote. For whatever it means when children judge their own mothers, I don't believe this was altogether a husband's loyal flattery. In practical comparisons she stood on the short side, but never required high heels to convince people she was taller, which she demonstrated by an erect graceful walk, like balancing one of her books on her head, and by looking everyone directly in the eye, as if equal to their height. My mother's name was Melody. She despised it, claiming, "A girl called Melody will never be taken seriously." Myself, I doubt she hardly needed to worry.

Her parents opposed the marriage to my father, because, as I mentioned once, his behavior tip-toed on a nervous edge after his military service, smoking and drinking, although my mother calmed him down, I guess, and I saw none of those habits when growing up. They decided it best to elope, driving off on their honeymoon in a twenty-year-old car for an adventure of tent camping in western states. This trip formed such happy memories my mother and father repeated it almost annually, missing the summer of my birth, plus one or two others.

These summer travels became my childhood highlights, not surprisingly. Away we would go, our merry band of three, already inside a family bubble of anticipation and delight, packed up, jammed up, inside a much newer and roomier vehicle now, carrying a palatial six-person tent, a four-burner propane strove, three overkill arctic (sweaty) goose-down sleeping bags with foam pads for underneath, a pantry of dried foods, ice cooler, several boxes with my mother's latest books. *Et cetera.* And the Beretta M9 handgun came along with us, should you be curious. My father had salvaged a single worn cowboy boot from somewhere, and he hid the gun inside, the ammo clip down at the boot's toe. Whether we overnighted at a motel or by our usual night in the tent, that cowboy boot had its place on the floor. I still today picture the droopy thing—rounded left at the heel, its top with a compensating tilt to the opposite side.

On what would be our last western road trip—when I was, nearly, a teenager—I remember clear as glass our particular stay at Turquoise River Campground. It had been a third return visit there. We reserved the same campsite, a pretty spot close along the river, where a rocky outcropping towered above a popular swimming hole. During our previous seasons I had watched the adults and older kids dive from those tall rocks into the river. That year I jacked up my courage and tried the jump myself. The first two dives were successful enough to encourage another, when I hit the water flat on my face, possibly breaking my nose, and lots of blood flowed, ending with twisted paper napkins stuffed up my nostrils for an entire afternoon. I refused to get teary unlike with my bicycle accident and my skinned knees. My father understood that I had gotten too old for Chicken or Egg distractions and he just clapped me sympathetically on the shoulder. But my mother. It was the Latin connection in Essay #12 that illogically caused me to recall this scene and her. My mother changed the paper napkin swabs and held my hand for most of that long achy afternoon. I had looked down at my blood drying on her hand. She must have misread my mind, since she said, "Think you're too old for your mom to hold your hand, do you? No, you're not. Not if I want to hold it. Not when holding your hand helps your mother feel better."

Actually my blood there on her hand had been the fascination for me. Red on white. My red on her white. Dr. B, think about it, about such an ugly red splotch on such a soft whiteness. That woman made it easy to love a mother.

I rattle on here. Well, I do want to insist that my mother would have been intrigued by you, Dr. B, as much as my father, and not to exaggerate at all I enjoy reading you through them both. And regarding the most current essays, and the Latin, I hear my mother's voice ringing out: "*COGITO ERGO SUM*. I THINK THEREFORE I AM! Descartes, my dearest!" Her repeating that was her solution to whatever doubts or moans I had, from the abstract to the personal. When younger, if I said, "I think my stomach feels sick," she might answer, "You think it, you'll be it, for you can't be it without thinking it. *COGITO ERGO SUM*, yes? Lay down in bed and we'll rub your belly." When I was older, after my smattering of physics lessons in school, I needled her by saying, "How do you know that I am an I and you are a you? For an undeniable proof?" She answered, "I could offer up my *COGITO*." And I said, "But your thinking of us could simply be an illusion of us." She had laughed and laughed, almost giggles—so unusual for her—and which I liked a lot.

To honor my mother, with her *cogito*, I let myself spend extra hours fumbling around in this topic of Mind versus Matter, or the physical world versus our world of consciousness, or possibly not a *versus* at all, but a unity. Dr. B, you wrote early on that it's not "mind over matter" but rather "minds matter." Should we rank Mind/Matter far up in your Top Ten Hit Parade of Final Question songs? And out of curiosity: Am I in charge of my own mind, or does it have a mind of its own? Aha, I just found our hit song title: "My Mind Has a Mind of Its Own, When I Think About Lovin' You." Perfect for the Country & Western market? (No, hold back those country horses! I'd promised myself no more thinking about Brown Eyes.)

I do my darnedest with Essays #10-#11-#12, because as you forcefully explain, what I make, when I think, is ME. Accordingly, I want three certain people to value ME: my dead father, my dead mother, the living Dr. Bartleby. Brown Eyes is also dead, metaphorically.

This specific Final Question must be a tough nut to crack—yes?—if as you suggested earlier we have no other choice to evaluate our minds except by utilizing our minds. Whatever is this "mind" exactly? Is the mind's "consciousness," launched from the mechanical energy of the brain, stuck forever there inside our heads, with its separate intangible version of reality? Will some major genius ever quantify consciousness in a mathematical formula? Will the busy quantum physicists ever weigh actual "thoughts" on a laboratory scale, like a pound of hamburger? Does every sentence I write on this wobbly subject have to end with a question mark, including this one? I hear my mother giggling again. "*COGITO*, darling!"

As a kid myself, to stare up into the blazing night sky amazed me beyond the powers of amazement. I grappled with any notion of such vastness with those trillions of galaxies and their billions or trillions of stars each. To apply another sidestep into your mother's Latin: **Omne ignotum pro magnifico**. *"What is unknown is always considered magnificent." Now, as an adult pomegranate farmer, I assign impressiveness of the physical universe to the primary fact of* **scale***, measurements beyond our human context, both in diminution (ever sub-atomic) or expansion (endless). Instead, in my adulthood, the unbounded human consciousness is what finally astonishes me the most. It, too, eludes any scale. Its complexity defies any schematics or science. You have heard me issue this same pronouncement before, and you will again. To explain it from another avenue:*

What you tell me about your family life, snippets here and there, mere snatches, is more enormous than the entire heavens.

*Analyzing what **thought** "is" brings out the same smell or suspicion of asking what **time** "is" or what **space/void** "is." All three have an unnerving abstraction about them, yet all three interact with the physical universe. Thought or consciousness even seems to spring from corporeal **us**.*

You betcha, this Body-Mind/Matter-Consciousness schism has battered Thinkers since way, way back, bruising them black-and-blue, ironically with sore spots on body and mind both. Should you wish to follow this quarrel over the millennia, brush up on classic Greek, your mother's Latin, and Fraktur German, before getting on to English. These would take you on your initial step. Or to spare us a lifetime of steps or study, we can streamline a brutally simplified overview: There has been the separatist camp, with its many variations, placing mental reality into its own idealized or spiritual or mystical or theological or psychological world. There has been the integrationist camp, with its many variations, mixing mind and body in assorted arrangements to explain an existential order. And there is the rationalist camp, also with its many variations, delineating reality according to logical systems that may decode mind/matter classifications as a fallacy altogether, or reality can best be explained by a reductive procedure, either mathematically, or anatomically, or in a scientific experiment discovered down in a "consciousness" or "god" quantum particle.

Before we ourselves jump into this philosophical mud fight, why not first try to answer the question you challenged your dear mother with, long ago? After all, unless we have confidence in trusting our own thoughts as real, why bother listening to them, since then we are only a self-ratifying illusion.

*Your mother repeated the venerable **Cogito ergo sum**—"I think therefore I am," a statement of Enlightenment assurance that along the centuries has reaped its ample quota of admiration and dismissal. For our purposes we stand beside your mother and posit a homemade corollary: "I will accept your thought that there is no existence, if you will admit that your thought exists."*

—If you do not admit it, you have erased your own assertion.

—If you do admit it, you have invalidated your own assertion.

This little pool of quicksand logic probably illustrates why your mom giggled. We know thought exists because it must. Like physical matter, consciousness is real because there are no other options. When we are left with an impossibility what remains is only the possible.

If thoughts are real, what do we mean by their "reality?" First, we should clarify that the reality of consciousness and the reality of concrete matter are equally valid, although they can function as independent realities, again with equal validity.

To illustrate this duality we place a philosophically famous cat inside a philosophically famous closed box. Unless the cat starts squalling inside, until that box gets opened an observer cannot confirm whether the cat is alive or dead. Meanwhile, in the mind of the observer, the cat consists of the mixed potential of "living cat" and "dead cat," potentiality itself being a legitimate conceptual reality. But this reality is not identical with the cat's unknown physical reality. Inside that box the actual cat is not both alive and dead at the same moment. This comparison of cats is another example of palpable reality (the irritated cat shut in the box) waiting to catch up with impalpable reality (the cat discovered in time, space, cognition).

Consciousness is wildly fleet of foot, conceivably (pun not disavowed) faster than the speed of light. Even our cat in the box has the potential—besides dead cat or living cat—of being a mistaken opossum—to be determined only when the box is opened and the animal is "quantified" by professional testing.

Of course the list of potential realities has no limit, whether applied to the cat or the observer of the cat. Extending this list too far returns us to where your mother would giggle again. We will just repeat: Uncertainty Principles do not equate with all outcomes being certain, nor with all events being certain at all points in time. Uncertainty, as the common term itself indicates, consists of a period of transition, of a measured span of ignorance, or of a procedure of discovery to phrase it more positively.

The conflicts between mind/matter often can be a byproduct of not only force-feeding one reality experience into the other reality experience, but by denying its reality completely. And, yes, before you ask, a sick man's hallucination of a two-headed monster is real, even if nobody else sees it in the room. Consciousness plays no favorites. Consciousness accepts all.

The bright sun here today and these heated ruminations have made me warm. My pomegranate trees and I need a drink of water.

Dr. B:

And your talk makes me thirsty, Dr. B! I do a lot of swallowing. My drinking must be slightly alcoholic because, lo and behold, after reading you I feel buzzed, light-headed, and more light in spirit than I can recall for a good while.

One idea, especially, attracts me. Essay #10 convinces me that our thoughts aren't mysterious ephemera isolated within ourselves. It convinces me that consciousness doesn't have to condemn us to loneliness. Just the opposite, consciousness can allow us to connect with what's outside us, consciousness-to-consciousness so to say, signaled by touches, by an exchange of glances, by a snuggle, a groan, a sigh, and supremely by language. Our words are a handshake between our minds. Don't you agree?

I know you agree, Dr. B. Your *Final Questions* and your answers to me are even (pardon my familiarity) more an embrace than a handshake.

An encouraging addition to this consciousness business is that it can leave a permanent record of its thoughts behind, constructing a one-way conversation from the past to the present. Considered along these lines the sensation feels ghostly, but what's a library full of books other than contact with the dead or soon-to-be dead? If my grandfather had written a diary, and I found his scribbled pages today, or tomorrow, he wouldn't be a vacant shadow to me, and I could give your Essay #4 a different answer.

No, I won't act dispassionate about voices from the past. The opposite is true and to a fault. I won't pretend otherwise. Surely by now you see through me, Dr. B, see me grabbing hold of my yesteryears with both hands, refusing to let loose.

Tonight the past is a letter from my father. He sent it after I went off to college—trying hard to stay a student—and he was at home, on yet another leave from work, with a long silence between us, while we tried to figure out any proper way to fill a deep family hole after my mother's death two years before. In the letter he avoids using the name Melody, honoring my mother's dislike of it maybe. Or possibly forming the letters M-e-l-o-d-y cut into him too sharply.

So tonight I sit here at my home desk supposedly reviewing a manuscript titled *The World of Window Boxes*, illustrated with 175 color photographs. Herbert my colleague is sold on the project, he has announced. But as usual tonight I have only one manuscript on my desk. Yours, Dr. B. And there beside *Final Questions* rests my father's letter to me, freshly exhumed from a scuffed carton of mementos I energetically abandoned until of late. Just as I sit here, right now, reading his letter again, he had sat at his desk writing it to me, "trapped in this house of memories, unable to avoid her face waiting in each room. I repeat our conversations together. I try to get the nerve, still after all this time, to remove her clothes from our bedroom closet. The notion of sorting through those clothes to donate away, and emptying the underwear out of her dresser for the landfill, makes me sick to the stomach. It does. I may sell the house, as an escape. Be prepared for that. Sure the memories will follow me, house or not, although who wants it any different I suppose, to lose the happy images in my head, but living here is tough, particularly walking into her room where we put the hospital bed. I apologize for bringing up all these bad things and am very sorry for my moping like this. You have enough to worry about without listening to your father complain. And you have your own hurt to deal with. I catch myself sniffling, mainly nights, how about you? Well, you never were the crying sort, much like your mother. I'll bet you can't remember her shedding a single tear, not once, not your whole life, am I right? Even during her last months we never saw any tears. Imagine that. Except, except, she cried on two occasions that you should know about. My telling, my remembering, puts me through a sentimental meat grinder, but I really need you to hear. On the first of those two times, your mother and I were sitting all alone in my old rusted-out Pontiac sedan, late at night, half of the moon bright, as I still can recall it, along with plenty of pretty stars, my arm around her shoulders, and I proposed. Her tears oozed and I tried wiping them with my fingertips but that just made a mess and made her cheeks shiny in the moonlight. On the second of the two times, you were in the delivery room, already present in person, while your eyes couldn't focus yet to see her tears. What a picture. You mewing and fussing on her bare chest, while she cried. So the woman who never cried from sadness or any pain cried to show how much happiness we gave her, you and I. And now listen to me carefully please. I want to explain the most necessary reason why I send this letter to you. I want you to realize that you loved your mother more than I did, which is not easy for me to set down on paper, because I cared for her above all else. You were the brave one between us. When she waited for us I ran away. Oh, I had my excuse, another overnight business trip, or such, but we both know the truth, that it was running away. You, so young yet, stayed. You refused to run. You proved your love. My biggest wish is that she understood my cowardice and forgave me. Also I want you to forgive me for leaving you behind alone. A father should never have done that. I can only tolerate myself if you believe, in your heart, how honestly you showed your mother your love, while I failed."

I warned you fairly, Dr. B, to prepare yourself for a major dose of emotional personal history—no extra apologies demanded from me I hope—and the letter does anyhow demonstrate my point, I feel, of how our thoughts have a method of materializing themselves and transferring between minds. Can you give me your approval of this idea, Dr. B?

I guess I require your support before trusting myself to trust my own head and what it wants to believe. Does that make sense? I have other basic questions about "consciousness" and how it varies, if any, from simply being "awake." Do my father's thoughts, captured in his letter to me, now exist only on this piece of paper, or do his thoughts also carry on somewhere else out in that endless universe you describe, Dr. B. And if I lose or burn this letter? "Nothing kills faster than forgetting kills," says Essay #4.

Give me more advice!

Another question for you. Can cats think? Really think? Like people do? I had an important cat once, and not a theoretical cat-in-a-box, but a genuine breathing tabby. "Spaghetti" we named her. She chose to leave with the brown-eyed person when the leaving time came. I had to speculate, "Why didn't Spaghetti pick me?" What decision or what judgment went on in that small brain of hers? Did she think, "Divorce hurts us all." Or did she think, "Goodbye, loser." In cat language.

I'm pleased to notice that I can poke fun at myself. Ha-ha?

----

*I appreciate that tamped-down smile of yours at the close of the last message. It **was** a smile, and not self-inflicted sarcasm? Let me stick with smile. Any talk about a cat called Spaghetti has got to end with a smile.*

Mostly I appreciate your decision to reread your father's letter and in the process read it aloud to me, via the printed word. You ask if this exchange between the three of us was a trustworthy example of "consciousness" out in the "real" world. To me, I must tell you, I found myself suddenly in the middle of a brightly lit room with the three of us standing there stripped naked. Is that real enough for you? Now relax and stay (figuratively) naked. Your father is/was real. His thoughts are real, and will remain real until you destroy them in the letter and in your mind, and I do the same in mine. You are real. I raise real edible pomegranates. Remember, we know we exist in a real world because we humans are late-comers to it. Keep naked, find other naked people. Find another (unboxed) cat.

Did the departing Spaghetti think about you when she went out the door? In a manner. Did she think about you with the depth that you thought about her? No. Does Spaghetti the cat have emotional feelings? Yes. Are these feelings as multi-faceted as yours? No. Is Spaghetti a creature with consciousness? Yes. Is her consciousness equal to yours? Absolutely.

For disagreement with me, what limits have Thinkers attempted to place on consciousness. What gradations have been put on its definition.

*—Starting at a **null** marker is the position already dismissed earlier in our essays, namely that consciousness is a human illusion, a phantom interior concept that we project onto an indifferent wall of external reality. Your father's letter, so considered, amounts to a card game of cerebral Solitaire. **Final Questions**, so considered, consists of no more than a reflection of my face in a mirror. Philosophy overall, so considered, is the unhealthy practice of academic masturbation.*

—Next on the scale comes the proposal that, indeed, consciousness does exist, but its quality can be reduced to the physical laws found everywhere in nature. For convenience we will simplify these laws as nature's "urge

to order" (or even to deliberate disorder). Accordingly, the behavior of atomic structures or the behavior of gravitational attractions, for examples, demonstrate a version of "aware" purpose—at a minimum, another version of Darwinian decision-making. Unfortunately, what is otherwise an admirable poetic instinct among certain physicists and other Thinkers takes the term "consciousness" and uses it as metaphor, mixing or confusing patterns of mechanical force with the patternless void that is consciousness. Darwin's collected scientific evidence, for instance, is not kept separate from the act of Darwin's conceptualizing. And at this juncture it would do no harm returning to Essay #1. We shall never see a star cry. Crying requires consciousness, as your father knew well.

—We can observe that not only advanced animal life responds with purpose to the world outside itself. Viruses fluctuate in and out of proliferation depending on their parasitic success. Plants function to maintain their existence, seek sun or shade, send roots after water and nutrients, protect themselves with thorns and toxins, have a plethora of reproduction devices. Following the most primary of storylines, plants live, and die, exactly as we do. But plants live a life without perception, incapable of comprehending their selfhood. This is life within a great blankness.

—Together with eternal time and space, eternal consciousness waits to be exploited: three impalpable realities that, as noted before, have a calculable meaning only when engaged by palpable matter or energy. All three exist without boundaries or restrictions and without requiring cause. When time, void, and consciousness are utilized, they are used totally. In other words, consciousness is either engaged, or not. And like space-time-process, awareness exists as an unchanging absolute, outside of alteration. A single distinction does divide these three infinite constants. A particular type of material matter is necessary to employ and exploit consciousness, and thereby recognize the other two companion impalpable realities. This required type of physical matter is a neural complex.

—At what point in evolutionary development an energy system—label it a neural network—first registered consciousness will never be known, nor needed to be known. That point (on planet Earth) happened long before human history, long before Spaghetti the cat and her precursors, long before Tyrannosaurus Rex and friends. Presumably far back, in our primordial sea, some tiny twitching thing connected with the fact of awareness. Yet—to remind ourselves—consciousness by itself is not intelligence. Consciousness together with informational input forms intelligence. The larger the neural storage capacity

the larger the thought capacity. A newborn infant is as conscious as an adult. Brain maturation combined with experience determines degree of cognitive perception.

On balance, I believe you can safely conclude that Spaghetti went on to remember you, and miss your scratching behind her ears.

Four

At the office I feel myself as something of a charlatan, properly arriving by 9:00 but spending too long studying the shifting clunk of the minute hand on the antique wall clock above Franklin McDermott's desk.

"Like a consult?" Franklin asks me, his encouraging smile primed and ready.

"No, no. Just thinking."

Herbie was hip-deep in the window box manuscript, obviously excited, for him, about it. "My goodness, look at these geraniums," he exclaims. "Let's make this photo a double-page spread." He looks over for my reaction. I have no reaction since I'm occupied matching up Herbie, Franklin, and myself with Dr. B's Essay #13, which I had re-read earlier this same morning while finishing a breakfast of fruits and cheeses. No pomegranates.

"Two-page splash," Herbie posits aloud, "or not? Too splashy for geraniums?"

If I considered Essay #13 soberly enough, might a whole book on flowers in window boxes be judged, by the universe at large, as trivial business? Was Herbie's enthusiasm about the book not much more than a happy child at play? Was Franklin, up there on his elevated desk, with his bald spot, the comic emperor of a kindergarten?

"I'll check on it in Essay #13," I tell Herbie.

Although I waited, he never bothers to crinkle his pale forehead and ask, "What Essay #13?" Could have been Herbie didn't hear me, already lost back into his window boxes. Or could be he finally figured out that I was the trivial one in the universe.

Essay #13

Calculating Odds That Humans
Are the Smartest Creatures Anywhere

Mirror, mirror on the wall, who's the fairest
of them all?

[Explication: Not you anyhow.]

Dr. B:

Essay #13? Early on I never acted much a futurist, never read much science fiction, but Brown Eyes was a huge fan. As a result we had our fair share of discussions, with me usually playing devil's advocate. Not arguments, we scarcely argued—even right down to the end when we divvied up our belongings we stayed polite. "Do you want the table lamps to go with you?" "Doesn't really matter. Maybe you want the table lamps?" "Take both if you want." "You take both if you want." "Where should Spaghetti go?" "Wherever you want." "You brought the kitten home." "You feed her most." "Wherever she chooses to go?" "Wherever." "Okay then." "Okay." "Goodbye then." "Goodbye then." It troubles me how wonderfully we got along. Probably quarreling now and again would have been better, or better at the end, when it mattered most. "No, I'm not saying goodbye. You say goodbye if you please. Not me. Not to you. And don't touch those ugly table lamps. I can't imagine why you paid 200 bucks for those two monstrosities, but they remind me of dopey you, so leave 'em behind."

Brown Eyes would go off on a romp with your Essay #13, Dr. B, like a kid ripping open a Christmas gift. I can hear the gush of enthusiasm.

"What? Humans not a big deal? Who after all conquered this whole planet Earth?"

"What? What? Compared to some alien Super Species are we the equivalent of Spaghetti the cat to us? Or worse, are we only as intellectually advanced as a snail?"

"So what form would any Superior Animal take? Or did it stop being an 'animal' as we define that noun? Instead more a machine, sort of alive and sort of immortal?"

"Think about it. Should we respect our extraterrestrial friend or fear our master?"

Nowadays, Dr. B, you and your essays lead me to wonder if any Lord of the Mind, from off in a far corner in space, at last has all the Final Answers to the Final Questions? (Which would send your book straight to the discount table!)

My vote, Dr. B, is that we (lowly) humans gradually improve into our own superior state, rising among the stars ourselves and ranking with the wisest of the wise. No, wait, Brown Eyes would cast that vote. I'm the devil's advocate, supposedly. I get to stay behind with us snails.

In these upper realms of hypothesis, one almost prefers being judged clever rather than a genius. A clever person is always recognized as clever, whereas the genius usually gets upended by another genius.

Much the same way, while human history has from time-to-time shown impressive genius, it reveals itself to be, to date anyway, basically an extension of our vanities. (The more polite terminology is homocentrism.) But why expect anything else? Is it shameful to insist on "knowing that you know what you know"? Hardly. Huddled around the earliest campfires, or before campfires, our ancestors saw the starry heavens wheeling past, felt and believed themselves at the centerpoint of a revolving spectacle. And in their conscious lives, they were.

*Now we are more informed. Now we view the heavens with different assurances. Yet we still believe in knowing what we know. Our question is, our doubt is, how **much** can these humans know to know.*

*Evaluated among all other animals currently found on Earth, the **homo sapiens** species distinguishes itself in very few categories, and in no category completely. Human subtleties and sophistication have added only various degrees of difference in the comparisons. Bear with me while I put down an obvious checklist.*

—*Humans have anatomical structures identifiable in other animals.*

—*Humans attract, mate, reproduce in actions similar to other animals.*

—*Humans, as omnivores, feed off companion flora and fauna life, exactly as other animals do.*

—*Humans have fundamental instincts of survival identified in other animals.*

—*Humans construct social organizations as do other animals.*

—*Humans develop tools as do other animals.*

—*Human seek to exploit their environment as do other animals.*

—*Humans have a conscious awareness that is also present in other animals.*

—*Humans can communicate, as do other animals.*

—*Humans are capable of cognitive perception and memory, qualities that exist in other animals.*

—*Humans have a finite lifespan, as do all animals.*

*The summary evidence of the above list? Plainly **homo sapiens** is not a unique life form. Granted, we have become highly specialized in certain limited fields of achievement due to a much more developed intelligence, but this is a comparative advancement and not a difference in kind. What we humans are, what we became as a species, obviously others elsewhere can become, if not exceed us. And the certainty that this fact of other life, of extraterrestrial life, has already happened can be statistically guaranteed beyond serious refutation. After all, our minuscule planet is only a brief beautiful bauble in the middle of an infinity.*

We ourselves, we current humans, exist as rank newcomers even by measurement with the first earthly life forms, let alone in geologic terms (a nod here to your father the geology student) where we arrived a literal minute ago. Being such newbies, could we in upcoming millennia evolve into our own Super Species, hardly connected to Spaghetti the cat?

First, by looking backward as far as possible before we look forward, what has NOT progressed about the "modern" human animal up to the present moment. Are there hints supporting, or perhaps discouraging, a "doctrine of evolutionary perfectibility"—a cheery theory popular in an earlier century— claiming that the world, through its natural selective mechanics, will inevitably produce units of improvement. Sorry, but now comes another list.

—Repeating here the position that consciousness itself equals a changeless and constant availability of awareness, then human intelligence at any stage, including the past, has had unlimited use of its memory powers.

—Repeating another observation, that basic **homo sapiens** *physiology has not altered over time, while diet, environment, and localized breeding have created surface variations.*

—Basic biological instincts have remained a solid human bedrock: preservation, procreation, domination. We want to live forever. We want to avoid hunger, avoid cold and heat. We want to win a mate. We want to collect more and more precious seashells. We want our neighbors and competitors to be more fearful of us than we are of them.

—Very unlikely it is, as well, that the human emotional range has ever expanded. Any feelings we are capable of today surely entered the minds and hearts of our predecessors, no matter how subtle the mood, and although these emotions can blend, their categories remain simple: all are shades of Happy/ Unhappy.

—And to repeat a final definition—that intelligence is the native ability to hold and manipulate information in memory—it would seem improbable to claim ourselves as improved models of humankind. Cranial capacity has not grown. Most significantly, every discovery of ancient text we find, or every sample of yesteryear's technology or art, all reveal an intelligence matched to ours. Every question in my Final Questions has been asked before ages ago. Our leaps to the moon and beyond have not come from getting smarter.

If no net increase in human capabilities is discernible, the advances we see around us in today's world must be credited to an increased amount of information that is arriving for our intelligence to utilize, and an increase in the methods this information can be saved and managed.

Everyone can recite the primary human story that allowed these informational advances: our slow journey from roaming hunter-gatherers to agrarian settlements to industrialization to specialized urban centers, ending with, and depending on, information harvesting being as vital as any food gathering. Crucial to this story was a developing descriptor system, those languages—spoken, written, mathematical, scientific—without which we could not identify nor preserve the increasing data our progress requires. (We will, almost, skip revisiting here the inherent counter limitation of how language restricts understanding "reality." That is, if it cannot be named, it cannot be conceived. For the present we keep on using language because we must.) Starting from an oral tradition isolated within tribal groups, language gradually regularized and expanded through social and trade contact, through a symbolized alphabet structure written by hand, through mechanized printing, through the universal digital medium, and stored over the generations in manuscripts, books, libraries, computer systems, data centers.

*However, be careful. See Essay #13 and beware of getting lost in our own fascinating mirrors. Massive data accumulation or not, we remain the same hunter-gatherers. For a modest illustration of that statement we compare two of our brightest human achievers from the past, Nicolaus Copernicus (died 1543) and Geoffrey Chaucer (died 1400). Copernicus was a mathematician-astronomer who solidified the heliocentric theory of how the earth revolves around the sun instead of the reverse, a view that ordinary folks (and scientists) thought nonsensical. Chaucer, himself a hobby astronomer, wrote the famous **The Canterbury Tales**, a literary milestone depicting in close detail English society during the Middle Ages. Copernicus, although brilliant, still had lots wrong with his astronomy, as* *current knowledge shows. Chaucer, over a century older than Copernicus, has today not a single part false in* **The Canterbury Tales** *with its picture of human nature. Such is the separation between our changing information about the universe and our unchanging selves.*

Dr. B:

Hey, Dr. Bartleby! Don't just screech to a stop in the middle of the race. Tell me, where do we hunter-gatherers go from here? Isn't there a finish line someplace up ahead we could aim for, improving our character along the way, instead of running in the identical place forever, like a caged hamster on an exercise wheel? I, for example, Dr. B, am not 100% satisfied with myself. Occasionally, I never like who I am, period. But what are my options?

To improve on the animalistic basis of our species, I imagine, means relying on the very same ballooning database of OUTSIDE info to invent procedures for changing INNER humanness. We appear to be underway, with this stem-cell wizardry and these genetically engineered creations we hear about. I, my humble self, can fantasize a utopia of zero disease and perfect health, where all individuals are required by law to report at age 200 for the death ceremony. Except what good is gained if people, everywhere, left and right, still hurt each other before reaching that age 200? What's gained if couples still go through 200 years of shock divorces with a repeated series of ugly table lamps and vanishing brown-eyed soulmates? Excuse, excuse, excuse my bringing up that reference again.

More important than an immortality gene is a kindness gene. If not more important at least as important, because disease is cruel, the opposite of kindness. And better, if we were always safe from harm who would need any Beretta M9 waiting up in the closet. Excuse that reference, too.

The fate of humanity resides in its own Petri dish. Is that a real answer? Or real craziness.

While I'm juggling ideas high over my head, I want you to take a few of them out of my hands before they fall down and injure somebody. Tell me what you conjure up in the way of superior extraterrestrial beings. Actual angels? Monster machines? Our rescuers, our saviors, our rulers?

I was just taking a breather. Final questions burn large amounts of oxygen. Are you nodding your head in agreement?

*Onward. Let us pick up our feet and follow your curiosity about an evolutionary high-water mark for **Homo sapiens**. In general we understand that other earthly species manipulated their gene pools to increase odds for survival, most notably by elimination of unhelpful breeding partners. We humans participated in that natural winnowing process, as discussed previously, until thousands of years ago we stabilized at our present and adequate body parameters. With billions of individuals populating the planet as proof of procreation success, our days of significant evolutionary challenge are over, or stalled. For now we obey the rule of regression to the mean. We swim in the genetic spittoon of the world's population.*

But as you rightly point out, humankind has recently put itself into a strange new world (for Earth) and become an architect of its own biology. What might we achieve with such unusual (for Earth) powers?

Probably not as much as you would wish, since your wishes are ultimately great. The hopes for almost perfect health, yes, certainly, that will come, given another five hundred years without civil or environmental disaster. Super longevity is slower business. By the year 3000, perhaps yes, if we reach that year 3000 unimpeded and solve the sequence to endless cellular regeneration. Along that road the questions would then be, how much prenatal invasive screening do we allow or demand, with how much slicing and dicing of defective genes, or whether we even bother with primitive in-body pregnancy, taking the safer shortcut to controlled birth laboratories. The questions also include how many self-powered artificial spare parts do we actually want to grow in the flesh factories and insert into how many billion people who function for what purpose other than to stay alive—and how many such interventions could we afford, whether financially or socially. Possibly these questions and others have positive answers. Possibly.

*I hear you thinking out loud that what you truly want is healthier people in another sense. You want that **kindness** gene, the **I-love-you** gene.*

Here is an animal tale for us to ponder. The ocean shark has had opportunity to evolve for 450 million years, surviving five mass extinction events that decimated our planet. Yet the shark stays today what it began as: a voracious predator. And likewise, regardless of how healthy the human body may become, or how long-lived, or in whatever celestial refuge it may escape to when Earth turns bad, it remains the human body, reacting within the boundaries of its nature. Boost our brain power to full retention of every datum it ever received, couple that total personal memory with the most expansive digital reservoirs we construct around us, and we attain an extraordinarily potent computing network, and an inventive one. But intelligence by itself is not wisdom, nor, definitely, any guarantee of kindness. Were we a world crammed top-to-bottom with rare geniuses, their emotional world would remain perfectly recognizable to us for its commonness.

Our future selves could indeed make a decision to extend our level of eugenics from physical health to psychological behavior. Risky? Oh, yes. Oh, you bet. But to control life on a planet about to explode with disunity or fatal conflicts, who can predict what risk is. And for a "superior" society, with "superior" conclusions about "proper" human virtues, who can defend what risk might be. Conceivably we already are the risky ones. Evidence of destructive violence is all around in our history, correct?

We future selves might be convinced to practice a version of genetic lobotomy. Begin by reducing, then removing, our neural centers of aggression. Try altering our glandular chemistry. Tamp down our excessive appetites and urges. Deactivate the sex drive. Be leery even of hunger, gagging at the picture of people once eating real meat. (Drinking pomegranate juice would remain acceptable.) The societal goal of these eugenics is to float inside a warm peaceful bath of emotional stasis, while hopefully, concomitantly, not inventing ourselves into oblivion.

*Not to let the air out of this ambitious prospect—only adopting your respectable role of devil's advocate—have you ever wondered how much we would miss unhappiness, or at least dissatisfaction? This suspicion is far from new. Without feeling dissatisfaction or guilt would I have written **Final Questions**? Doubtful. Without loneliness would you have loved Brown Eyes, married Brown Eyes, hope to find another Brown Eyes? Doubtful. Does frustration promote inventiveness? Can fear do the same? Is unbroken contentment stifling? Might crude selfish ambition open paths to public benefit? And to sound more dramatic, are destruction and crisis a necessity, a handy crucible to forge evolutionary resets? And to exceed even the dramatic, do we require unavoidable, unpredictable death in order to place genuine purpose and worth on precious life? On and on.*

We humans will muddle ahead over the centuries, I suppose, keeping our fingers crossed for good luck, building denser and denser complex structures—both mechanical and social—and trying to keep a lid on the bubbling pot that is the individual **Homo sapiens***. The evolutionary directional arrow most critical would be how successfully those individuals build an organization among themselves, rather than any organic changes within the physical human animal. Such an evolution refers to categories of our lives currently at an early developmental stage: political governance, cultural cohesion. This means, specifically, essential issues of commonality, a worldwide unification from the simple (language) to the complicated (values). A sentence and topic like that major mouthful requires its own Final Question down the road.*

That was another breather pause. Now we can lean back and continue with the fun part, by musing about other intelligent beings existing out in the Otherness of the universe.

Duly note that I do not ask **whether** *intelligent life exists outside Earth. To deny or resist this certitude is a painful human vanity. I blush at any boasting about our uniqueness, much less claims of superiority. We love our tiny planet, understandably, and we love ourselves, predictably, but allow us, please, finally* *to put away this child's perspective that we alone are favored among the heavens.*

Reviewing the limitless process of time, reviewing the limitless rearrangement of matter over that limitless time, we are left with a conclusion that, already, there have been limitless cycles of life preceding us. These cycles, along their journeys, would have reached a wide range of intelligence.

*But to restrict ourselves to the observable present (a visual "present" itself representing billions of years in age) we can apply the most pessimistic storyline for potential life and find where it leads us. Assume that 99.9% of all planetary bodies in the cosmos are uninhabitable for any life form whatsoever. Assume that 99.9% of all habitable planets are eliminated by volcanic convulsions before intelligent life can develop. Assume that 99.9% of living matter does not progress to consciousness. Assume that 99.9% of intelligent life destroys itself after advancing to the **Homo sapiens** level. Now, despite the grand total of these negative assumptions, the enormity of the universe nevertheless guarantees the manifold existence of life elsewhere, and of intelligent species having had an evolutionary span that surpasses our relatively modest number of years. For the sake of argument—why not have an argument?—place ourselves, **Homo sapiens**, at the one-quarter mark on the progressive scale of* *maximum development of a species. And by development, I refer to the fullest understanding and utilization achievable of nature, of self, of technology.*

For the sake of other arguments, what do we end with if a remarkably blessed cognitive species, somewhere, survives to reach the finish line of the developmental scale, keeps chugging forward, like our ocean sharks, over 400 million years. We speak here of those potential Super Beings you speculate about.

As you probably suspect, never count me as one of those sci-fi illuminated minds who imagine that Super Beings will evolve into gelatinous brain globs floating in pots of permanent nutrients, being serviced and served by legions of androids. My guess is, rather, their appearance would not have changed dramatically throughout the mega-anni. Those original useful tool-making appendages would have stayed the same (our ten? their twelve?). That necessary and beloved ocular vision would have stayed the same (our 130 million retinal cells? their billion?). Our Super Beings, let me guess, will still use toilets, although what a toilet is, and what sewage is, might differ considerably from here on Earth now. Perhaps the sewage is also the food. Apologies, but that concept would simplify the circuit. I intend with these descriptions to emphasize that while our Super Beings would be impressively smart, and scarcely resemble us strictly, they would be recognizable and familiar to us as a functional life form, and their shape would not have morphed itself into something radically different.

Not necessarily equipped with an intellectual capacity beyond ours, the Super Beings do sit atop a Mt. Olympus of recorded knowledge earned over millennia of successful survival, that social survival serving as the springboard to all other advancements. They have had the peaceful space to establish a technical cyber-wonderland, but not a fantasy world. While they will live within a wholly integrated architecture of creature and machine, never will they travel through multi-dimensions across the galaxies to visit us, never reassemble their own bodily atoms, never slip inside time warps to visit their dead grandfathers and bring them peanuts or coffee. Only the reality of the imagination achieves these goals. Is that triumph enough?

We, too, on Earth, find ourselves in a period when science and technology appear always accelerating, and without boundaries. Except in our enjoyable excitement I suspect we overlook history and logic. The pool of attainable concrete knowledge, unlike the pool of pure creativity, is finite. Development surges, then decelerates. Super Beings may not totally suction out and empty the bottom of the information pool, but its depth will become shallower and shallower. Ultimately, off in the most remote of futures—should any species arrive at that future—a major instinct of their wonderful restless mental energy will diminish: "What new stuff is there to discover outside?" Instead the communal energy can concentrate again on the oldest instinct: "What should make us happy?" Hopefully this focus supports a state of equilibrium and not a descent into confusion or entropic boredom.

Five

Dr. B:

I wonder if any of those twelve-fingered Super Beings with their triple-rainbow retinas might have brown irises. At least the cyborgs or anyway the robots could have brown eyes? Darn it, this brown eyes addiction has worn me out. I give up. I quit with the Soul Sickness display. But for a public service announcement, I'll report that Brown Eyes has a new family with an eighteen-month-old daughter. She plays with Spaghetti or pulls its tail or both?

Tonight I choose to make myself groggy by thinking about AI (artificial intelligence) and your not-so-strange future beings, and my own not-strange-enough future, which is already here, not even a tomorrow away. This AI, I read, should pile up here soon and help us poor humans with, well, everything, from monitoring our vital body organs to telling us when our supply of toilet paper is low—and notice, Dr. B, how superbly I tie my thoughts back to your discussion of sewage.

Let me state, resolutely, I can imagine how much you dislike grogginess, and silliness and sentimentality, all on show by me tonight. With any good sense, I won't click the send button for this message, Dr. B. I just need a clue about where a person buys a quick supply of this sensibleness.

Seemingly, grogginess wins, and I retreat back to AI. Could the doctors ever plant a mood chip in my skull, an anti-sadness trigger mechanism that automatically releases a shot glass of dopamine in my brain? It would regulate my happiness as steadily as a pacemaker does the heart, regardless of outside events. Okay, I can see how this happiness trickery would be cheating, if anyone cares about that, and might be cheating in an invisible way, more dangerous even than the upfront use/abuse of happiness pills or alcohol. I suppose this sneaky invisibility justifies the nervousness about AI. It could prove easy to mistake, or worse to accept, that the artificial intelligence whispering in your head is your own human intelligence speaking.

And yes, I remember what you underscored, Dr. B, on how the day I stop complaining, and stop wishing, becomes the day I anesthetize myself into a permanent intellectual slumber. Any such so-called satisfied person wouldn't interest you, and not me either. Strange how that goes. Still, I do yearn for a future earthly world, a better world, where any Super Beings needn't feel sorry for me over my discomforts. How about a world, say, without victims of any sort, a world without impossible decisions to make, murderous decisions, a world without a Beretta M9 up in a closet waiting for a step stool—could AI give us that world? Could Super Beings teach us how to make one?

Am I actually going to send this groggy message? No.

Yes. You did. And you did exactly right. Enough said.

*I plead to everyone that we never depend on artificial intelligence to save our emotional souls. Let AI help save our literal sickly hides, simplify our routine lives, rescue our planet, expand our science, but not become our champion. The insidious risk of AI is not that it will grow all-knowing, all-powerful. The danger is that we ourselves grow to **believe** so, believe it wiser than us, believe we must depend on its final calculations, and let those calculations rule. The absolute danger threshold will be crossed when our holographic computers—with their depthless quantum data chambers—are allowed to program and reprogram themselves, while we humans stand aside.*

Reread Essay #1. Yet again. Turn back to the front. "Explaining Humanity in 2⅔ Words." Stars can't cry and AI will never cry either. No matter how many feedback loops you tie together inside the machine, no matter how godly complex the algorithms fed into its immortal plasma guts, all of that produces only simulation. In the lonely dark of the night a heart-felt voice—in exact Brown Eyes tones—may reassure you "I miss you, too," but the voice, and the heart, are fake. We will not label them lies, because lying requires a conscious intention, or personal judgmental motive, and machines lack the living avenue to consciousness. We do label the voice fake in the human context, meaning faux, which clarifies and reminds us of the key term, of the two words, in "artificial intelligence." And beware of those critical moments during the ongoing course of human time when AI turns plain stupid. At those threatening moments we trust our own intelligence wakes up.

With Essay #1 close at hand, we can use that highly truncated piece to illustrate further why stars and AI are closed systems, unlike humble human creatures who are wide open to the unpredictable and the original.

A rudimentary computer analysis of the Essay #1 title— which claims that the sentence "Stars can't cry" contains "2⅔ words"—would swiftly inform the author of his counting error.

"Stars can't cry" holds at a minimum three whole words, or four, depending on how the contraction "can't" is unpacked: "can not" or "cannot." So how to explain this goof-up, this erroneous "2⅔"? The author must have taken the spelling "cannot," removed those two letters replaced by an apostrophe, leaving behind four letters out of the six, therefore two-thirds of a word. However the helpful computer has registered this presumed slip as illogical, as a mistake, because a fraction of a word would be no word, merely a few nonsensical letters.

Nonetheless to the author "2⅔ words" is no mistake, or better, was a deliberate mistake, with the goal of causing an effect greater than "3 words" ever could. From the get-go, the essay's title rings the reader's bell. Clear your mind! Explain humanity in two and two-thirds words? Whatever the nonsensical "two-thirds of a word" logically fails to means, its creative point should be plain: a definition of "humanity" is so simple or obvious that the writer refuses to waste a full third word on it.

*The challenge: How to instruct a computer to learn when a **false** might be a **correct**, a **correct** might be a **false**, the **false** that had been **correct** on one day might stay a **false** on another day, or that **correct** could turn to **false** and **correct** again on the same day, and that **false** and **correct** might be identical all at once, or be both **correct** and **false** but to different degrees, as* *in Essay #1. For an additional challenge, each **false** and each **correct** can be dependent on each individual perceiver of the information.*

We have barely begun, ladies and gentlemen.

—The human reader of Essay #1 will consider its definition of "humanity" and absorb any implications. This process can last from one minute to one lifetime.

—The reader notes the author's intentional twist of logic in the essay's title and evaluates its effectiveness. Subsequently the reader tries on for fit the entirety of the author's creative style, and theme, like testing a pair of gloves for comfort.

—After sifting through the author's rhetorical skills and labors, the reader remembers that an actual person waits behind the words, who wishes mightily to break past the paper and grab the reader's attention, along with the reader's good will. The sensation seems sort of eerie. The reader might sneak a peek at the book jacket for a photograph of the writer. The reader visualizes the mysterious author hard at work at a study desk, a concentrated frown on his brow, or holding a ruby-red pomegranate, a concentrated smile on his lips.

—The reader begins, haphazardly, taking a shot at a personal version of "Explaining Humanity," aiming for a

record brevity. After thirty words instead of three, the reader stops, grins, sends the author a wave of respect. More seriously, more slowly, the reader unravels strings of ideas from a big abstract ball of yarn named "humanity." This teasing of loose ends can last from two minutes to two lifetimes. (Hold on! "Two lifetimes" is illogical again.)

—Abstractions about this "humanity" conception soon particularize into real humans and real stories, sagas fresh in the memory, shards from the shadows, laughter and sobs, bravery and flight, tender strokes and blunt rejection, kisses and spit, friends and strangers, fathers and mothers. For the reader this retrieval process has no end, and the data download is never completed.

*—Now the reader of Essay #1 realizes the best explanation of "humanity"—a one-word answer, shorter than the author's "2⅔" words. The reader, the **me**, is what any star or any AI machine can't/can not/cannot duplicate.*

And finally, while signing off on our Super Being colleagues out there in the far wilds of space, I would judge, in disappointment, that we shall not meet up for a chat. If we did, no doubt they could grant significant benefit to us, with their mighty technology, their social experience, and they could entertain us with their unusual and sophisticated arts. Also I would judge—

*with confidence—that **Homo sapiens** need not feel shame in front of our prospective visitors. Regardless of how great their achievements, our friends would not have heard any music superior to that composed by Ludwig van Beethoven, nor read any poetic juxtapositions more startling than Emily Dickinson's, shown no dedication deeper than yours for your mother. Cheers for our team.*

Essay #14

Should We Bother with Parenthood?

"Happy Birthday to you! Happy Birthday to us!"

[Explication: What's good for you is best for me.]

Dr. B:

Guess what, Dr. B. My feelings tell me that I want my own eighteen-month-old daughter or son. Apparently I do have "feelings," otherwise I wouldn't bump into the same ones most days when my mind should be on professional matters, like reading somebody's eager manuscript about Chrysanthemum Propagation or about Sweet & Sour Favorites. In the middle of this somebody's opus I suddenly remind myself how the editor (me) is also advancing through the biological zones of aging, and the editor is childless. Why does this bother me. Because it does. Am I jealous of Brown Eyes? Do I want a little Me Doll to play with? Do I, as much, want the mate who makes the doll with me? Is there an immortality instinct commanding me to cast my genes into the future void, like my author with his chrysanthemums?

After thinking long and hard, I believe part of my baby wishes is to replicate for my own kid the carefree life I had as a child, or more precisely the earlier years of that life, before my fourteenth birthday. I'm precise about the time, Dr. B, since in hindsight I can now interpret the particular week when one of the warmest family experiences I ever had as a child got jumbled with one of the coldest. I'll explain that to you, Dr. B. Suffering, very patient Dr. B.

Close to age fourteen, in the month of April, I spent most of a week with my father on one of his regional business trips where he reviewed company office procedures, or whatever he did. "Too tedious to describe to myself, let alone to you," he would claim. I skipped four days of school to go with him. Turned out he had skipped workdays to spend them with me. "We'll be bad for a few days. But we'll be bad together."

Meanwhile my mother took advantage of our absence to visit her own mother—my grandmother—who was having a severe bout of shingles. Off and away we went, my dad and I, and already in the car there was a special closeness building between us, with an unknown adventure waiting ahead as we explored our rule-breaking badness. In actual fact, although the adventure might be unknown to almost-fourteen-year-old me, my father did have a plan, and a goal. And it happened that after a short half-day stop at one of my father's field offices, and after he made a show of settling some work duties, our journey continued westward through the farmlands of Indiana, aiming for an obscure countryside townlet named Mason's Mill. "I grew up there," said my father. "Or I did until about your age." When I asked him why we hadn't gone there before, he said, "I don't really know."

On the first night underway we stayed at a grimy wayside motel and ate dinner in its grimy attached cafe. I remember my father griping about the combined griminess but I didn't mind. To me, it was novelty and excitement, traveling into strange territory, being alone with my dad and his treating me more like a grown friend instead of a child, which was another kind of strange territory that I enjoyed a lot. The next day we arrived at this Mason's Mill, a diminished place that had lost its place in the world when a bigger road bypassed it decades before. Out on that bigger road we checked into another motel, called Sleep-Ezee. "Look at that asinine name," pointed out my father. "I've had to sleep in a hundred of these Lysol-smelling boxes. The staff folks are always pleasant but just try to find a decent mattress that doesn't cripple your backbone. Now you know another reason why I hate to leave home."

I'm babbling here, Dr. B, babbling again. You brought up the topic of parenthood and this whole week spent with my father has forced itself into my thoughts and off I go, babbling. Yesterday I even questioned poor Herbie about his childhood. He stammered out several coherent answers. I only wish that, by this point Dr. B, you've developed calluses against my loose mouth. Please take these uncontrollable memories as a compliment to the effectiveness of your *Final Questions*.

Headed from the hotel back toward Mason's Mill, with a free afternoon on our hands, my father believed despite those decades that he could drive straight to his childhood home, if it still existed. It did. Shortly beyond the edge of town, down a crunchy gravel lane, stood a humble farm bungalow with peeling white paint and a ragged pattern of water stains on the roof. The front yard had more weeds than grass. Beyond the house, farther down the slope, trees with the fresh green of spring curved along the banks of a winding stream. My father sat in the car, quietly, nodding his head. Eventually he said, "Here's the home . . . definitely. The absolute same as before, minus the wear and tear and neglect. I played many hours down there in Mason Creek. During the 1850s a Mr. Mason built his flour mill along this creek somewhere, nearer the town."

We knocked on the door, although it seemed obvious that the house was vacant, probably abandoned. A couple of storm windows lay on the ground with their glass busted out and in the backyard a rusty tricycle rested upside down. My father assumed that a long line of renters—of descending standards and means—had worn his home down to the point of uselessness. "I could find the owner and buy it," he said, not sounding peevish, only thinking aloud, or dreaming aloud. We tried peeking inside but all the shades were drawn down, disappointing my father.

Instead we sat on the veranda while he described the interior layout for me. Then we went on sitting there, side-by-side, not saying much, or not saying a thing, watching a late afternoon breeze stir the leaves on those trees along Mr. Mason's creek. It was a fine afternoon for me.

That night in the motel we kept each other amused by sorting out the details of our day, and like the afternoon, it was a fine evening for me. The following morning, to my surprise, we weren't finished with our visit to the boyhood home. My father bought and assembled a tote of picnic food, and after parking the car beside the old house again we spent hours hiking the banksides of the creek. He had a few tales to tell, my father, whenever he recognized certain locations—a favorite hideaway, a summer swimming hole, a flooded cornfield, the spot where he first kissed a girl (Becca Chamberlain, two years his senior). "However," he said, "I never gave a rat's ass about any girl or woman until I met your mother." And I said, "Wow, a real glamorous comparison. Rats." That broke us both up. At the end of our hike, when walking up to the car, our hands somehow joined, unusual for a father and a budding teenager, except not on that afternoon.

During the evening in our motel room my dad asked me what I thought about returning for a final visit to the house and going right inside. Whatever did he mean, "right inside"? He meant "breaking in, like a pair of thieves." I had to question if, shucks, it was a crime? "Naturally," he told me. "We're being bad already—let's be a tiny amount badder." This was my father talking, and I couldn't figure out the why of this bad and badder business, not until we did it.

In the morning, after procrastinating through a late breakfast, we kept to the criminal intentions and once more crunched down the gravel driveway and parked by the scruffy old house, no one in sight, quietness everywhere. We scouted around the building to check the windows, found them all unlocked, and my body being the smallest and most agile my dad boosted me up, through a rear window, into the house. I stood there—before going to open the front door—stood there in the hazy sunlight of a bedroom with a bed's bare box springs tipped against a corner, and I could almost touch the ghost shapes of many lives passing by, including my father's. Then he, my real father, began rapping on the outside door. Together we circled though the stripped hollow rooms, our voices made foreign by their flat echo. My father had an anecdote for every room. In the kitchen we stopped. Unsurprisingly no water ran from the sink faucet, which my dad took as a major symbol of disappointment or loss, and he never mentioned again about buying his old home.

Yet he was glad to be here, he said with emphasis, and the best part of all was to stand here with me, both of us the same age in a way, his past and my present "linked together in one spot, child and child and father." That abstract picture is the most fanciful language I ever heard him utter.

Our last night in the motel turned extremely traumatic for a young person already on tip-toes from guilty trespassing. About bedtime (we had on pajamas) our motel door flew open and in barreled a large man who even resembled a shaggy barrel, shouting "What-the-hell-you-doing-in-my-place," knocking over a floor lamp. After more of his shouting I at last translated him as accusing us of being in his ROOM. Further, he proved to be blind drunk and staggering into furniture from loss of balance more than from anger. My father tried to convince the barrel guy of his drunken mistake but couldn't penetrate the yelling, forcing my father to use his Marine muscles—to grab and read our intruder's key number—and herd him outside into the next room.

For long afterward we heard him over there ranting a lengthy list of profanities. My father said, laughing, "Here's your chance to broaden your vocabulary. You didn't miss school after all." No laughing for me. My heartbeat refused to settle down and I actually asked permission to scoot my bed up against my father's, and this as a proud teenager. With the lights out, in darkness, I shut my eyes, although none of that eliminated the rumble of our neighbor's energetic swearing. In time I obscured the noise by concentrating on the steady relaxed breathing of my father. Oh, I was happy to have a father by me in this drunken world.

In that dark I said, mainly to myself, "Where's that Beretta M9 when we need it."

From the silence I thought my father had fallen asleep, before he did speak. "You and I don't need any gun here."

"We don't?"

"The Beretta is for when I'm not around. Remember?"

"Like at home?"

"Like at home. You remember."

"To protect Mom?"

"To protect you and your mother. You remember how. You want a review? Let's review and take our minds off our friend over there. First, fill clip. Put clip into gun. Clear your head. Pull back bolt. Safety off. Clear your head again. Aim with conviction. Squeeze don't jerk. We'll practice at the range."

Returned into the silence of our darkness, I could hear that my father had lost his relaxed breathing, and I blamed myself for mentioning the Beretta and making him agitated. But it wasn't the Beretta. Or not directly the Beretta.

I had nearly drifted asleep myself when my father began talking again, without any preamble, and his zombie voice in the blackness tipped our week's wonderful adventure over on its head.

The voice next to me said, "Your mother didn't go visit because your grandma was sick. The other way around. The sick person is the other way around. Don't worry, we'll work it out, the three of us. We will." My father was wrong about that, Dr. B, and whether he lied or was only wrong, I could never guess, then or now.

Motel Sleep-Ezee didn't live up to its name. My dad tossed and thrashed. The dark felt heavy as lead. On that night I began knowing, and today I know 100%, how my father's trip to his boyhood home amounted to a maneuver away from the punch of my mother's news. And he had used me, his young child, for security, for a protection not much different from my scooting my bed up to his. Dr. B, I gave my help just by existing, simply by being alive, being his child. I was willing to be used, even when sad myself, and despite that hurtful night, or because it was a hurtful night.

My story demonstrates, I think, Dr. B, an agreement tucked inside parenthood and an agreement with your Essay #14: "Happy Birthday to us." Families build a joint project where sometimes the kid gets to play the parent.

Well told. You definitely are your parents' faithful and caring child. And I repeat, out of respect, you might consider shifting a certain amount of your editorial skills from chrysanthemums over to biographies. I sense a powerful family story waiting for your guidance to be heard.

I admire your appreciation of your parents. Fortunate are those children who can innocently harvest the security of their childhood. In truth, in sadness, only children who possess this safety never suspect the chance of its loss. On the contrary side, a child living with anxiety or loneliness learns early about the fear of falling, a fright beyond physical injury, deeper than the threatening forces of any other circumstance, even hunger. When you hold a baby its fingers will grip your hair or your clothes or your own fingers. This instinctive action includes that literal fear of falling, plus ever more fear over the growing years: hold me, protect me, belong to me, teach me, never desert me, make for me a secure place in the giant world—and I can survive anything. Anything.

*A child easily recognizes whether it possesses a worth to others. And a child will naturally adopt that worth, internalize its value, a value beyond the level of bare ego, will use it as a shield against self-doubt or self-defeat. Nor is some ideal model of parenthood required to provide any such support—no—and we could use our own parents as examples with assorted flaws, no doubt. But our family essentials were solid. We wanted them to be our father and mother and they, in reverse, wanted to be the father and mother, demonstrating we formed a correct match regardless of those side imperfections. We felt reassured that we were, and would remain, part of their family, which became our protected private sphere. As a result, we understood why we deserved a place on that big stage outside of us, since somebody already considered us worthy, and had gifted us that fundamental **worth** for future life.*

Once again, I accept not the slightest originality for these remarks. Our good sense tells us how indispensable the snug blanket and warm arms and kind words are to the baby and child to form any successful adult, regardless of life's challenges. Yet governments spend boatloads of money, too late, to rescue what is already lost. Money, we find on the whole, cannot buy a healthy culture or repair broken parents. Up to this point no government has thus succeeded. To date the opposite has been the case, with evidence showing that only sound cultures build sound governments.

To my mind, the true heroes must be those children who survive parental failure or actual parental abandonment and end strong nevertheless. They are dropped. They fall. For some fortunate reason they do not shatter. They defy permanent harm because, perhaps, chance leads them to a powerful mentor or to the key words in a book or to a rare indomitable independence. Regrettably such survivors are the exception. To fall yet keep yourself whole demands unusual insight and grit, and children should never be required to save themselves.

Can we devise a better system for raising children than our traditional family unit with its risks and inconsistencies? As every analysis concludes, when the divorce rate rises—as it has—and where a child is born into a single-parent home, or no real home, that child steps into a deeply disadvantaged cavity. Back to our question: Can Mother State and Father Government fill in the hole that botched parenthood leaves behind?

To answer the question more accurately we should look ahead and calculate what "state" and "family" might become.

Consider a future where the worldwide birthrate falls below the population replacement number of one surviving child per adult, giving a negative growth rate already increasingly present in certain developed nations. Consider a world where families duplicate yours and mine—single-child families—due to a combined list of feasible causes:

—The impossibility of an unplanned pregnancy. Medical science, we will assume, develops a permanent chemical sterility switch, made a legal international health requirement for every prepubescent male. With approval the switch can be reversed to a temporary OFF position when conception is planned. (Any imaginative contraception specialist out there please be welcome to invent a superior version of this inevitable population control.)

—The trend of today becomes the fixture of tomorrow. Following a strong current of social forces, average family size dwindles with childless couples becoming common. These pressures include practical economic ones such as the familiar need for joint income, and subjective ones, such as commitment to personal development instead of developing children. A model to emulate for the fashionable modern couple would be the pair that proves it is not a baby-making arrangement. Couples with two or three children might feel

required to explain themselves to friends, with a degree of apology.

—The old Malthusian prediction of world overpopulation finally does materialize. However the tipping point is not food shortages, not disease, but psychological fatigue at the crushing weight of twenty or forty billion other people around you. This overpopulation suffocates individual breathing space (quality of private life) and leads to many flashpoints of conflict. As a consequence government would intervene with laws limiting family size as a key antidote.

—Environmental breakdown. Our badly abused middling planet has had all of the human species that it can stomach. Same antidote, same law: "Unless permitted under Penal Code Exceptions, Section 3383b, the Sterility Switch is allowed deactivation only ONCE."

—On a more (much more) basic level, the elemental progeneration impulse comes to be viewed as incompatible to an advanced human future, and the whole messy biological business of obedience to your pituitary gland, ordering you to reproduce, seems demeaning. (This somewhat uneasy topic surfaced during our discussion of Essay #13, on modifying human intelligence, if you recall.) At some developmental trigger point along the road of enlightenment

*all concept of romantic idealism is severed from sexuality—an earlier transitory type of enlightenment had injected romance **into** sexuality—and now the propagation/birth process will at last turn into a controlled laboratory procedure, without the genetic risks and outright discomfort of it being locked inside the body, like a pair of breeding livestock.*

All right. For whatever reasons, and there are many: one family, one kid. Or no kid. In short order the world population will halve, and halve again, until at a particular stage a nervous government intervenes yet again, now with measures to stabilize loss at an "optimal" level, potentially via a rewards system, potentially by total human laboratory reproduction, either outcome following strict genetic quotas for health, gender, and various other diversities. We might imagine the political bloodshed behind these formulas.

With world population held in a stagnant balance a substitute marketplace would have to be developed, one not dependent on an expanding consumer base. Let us accept that this different type of economy is achieved. Societies change—if slowly—and faster when survival demands it. Any new economic theory is a separate discussion and our subject here concerns another issue, the question of what to do with these newer, fewer babies.

Would children become more precious, more valued? Would we parent them any better than you and your father at Mason's Mill?

*To supersede the traditional parent-child bond the human animal would need to unlearn or subvert the basic physiological and psychological instincts that normally accompany a birth. Protective hormones gush, possessive jealousies rise, defensive powers elevate—the baby is so helpless, so cute, so **ours**, and besides (whispers a hidden voice) the species must continue. Nonetheless, humans are an unusual animal, one that can understand, and sometimes tame, its instincts.*

While there exist a limited number of advanced animal species that practice different degrees of group parenting, and an even more limited number of human societies that historically/ presently do full communal child-rearing, these essentially amount to workshare agreements, mutual arrangements that free up time for other activities, usually to service other practical necessities. This "delegating of parental duties" is not much removed, or not at all removed, from the current proliferation of nursery schools, preschools, day schools, play groups, summer camps, where children live lives away from their factual parents. But this broad middle ground of public quasi-parenting is not at all a sufficient replacement for the father-mother-child relationship. Society would have to do better. Society must soothe that innate fear of falling.

We can then project a future world where at birth—or at whatever that moment of arrival might be termed—the newborn is placed inside an elaborate societal system where its needs for security and reassurance are met, while avoiding any potential shortcomings of an individual mother or individual father. How to accomplish this? Perhaps by professional nurture centers, where highly trained staff guide the developing little beings along a careful path that bypasses the classic sort of particularized parental bonding, and replaces it with an attachment to the greater group.

At these nurture centers the babies rotate constantly, day and night, between variable teams of caretakers, specialists selected to represent a changing mix of gender and physical characteristics. (Once again, imagine the programmatic dance behind designing this social formula.) The babies are held and rocked by a sequence of different cradling arms, smiled down at by a careful variety of happy faces, spoken and sung to by a multitude of tender voices, snuggled and kissed by dozens of passing figures—all varying from the young to the elderly. The entire process intends to transfer the loyalty of children from the narrow and undependable circle of parents/family to the reliable support and purposes of the whole community. Every child begins life with an equal start. No child is ever abused in either body or psyche.

As the child grows older, its routine integrates into a rising contact with other children, around-the-clock youth assemblages where joint living and joint decisions are an expected norm. The mission of schools becomes classroom achievement and not individual success. Competitive sports fall out of favor. Teenagers feel it sensible to "fall in love" with multiple partners. Or our present notion of "love" will itself be redefined and rejected as egocentric selfishness.

In this future children everywhere reach adulthood imprinted with the same stable set of values, those precepts of behavior having been judged over time to be best for them, the children, and reflexively, best for society in general. Such a society with this unified behavior and beliefs—providing comfort to all and the fairness of uniformity—also does require a concomitant regimentation, a consent to the majority view, with a conceivable threat to personal freedom if viewed by today's westernized standards. But the world would be a safer place. And we, today, could be victims of a relic idea called parenthood.

I needed another escape, another walk, among my pomegranate bushes. A whiff of nature clears the head sometimes.

During my walk I asked myself: Can one child have a thousand mothers? A thousand fathers? Can your nation, your entire international world, be your family? Why not. It appeals. It represents the culmination of a respectable ideal, the final expansive goal closeted behind the likes of the League of Nations and the United Nations. And unified political theories of Central State or Single System share this goal, such as, in our own modern era, Marxist doctrine and its assorted adoptees. All these indivisible master governments, in practice, will be threatened by any competing loyalties, whether that loyalty comes from divergent cultures, or from the distraction of other specific social structures including religion, or ultimately, the separate family.

*Can any system of master rule—for instance, nationhood—actually replace **parenthood**? Why are tears disproportionately shed when a mother or father dies, we might ask ourselves, for starters. Apparently we should step back farther yet and ask for a fundamental definition: What **does** make a mother and a father for us humans?*

*At the biological level it begins as with other animals. We march along the standard maturational route of hormonal benchmarks, reach puberty, produce gametes, get prompted by nature to share deoxyribonucleic acids, wait out gestation, until **voilà**, parenthood. A deeper layer behind those purely mechanical imperatives we can categorize as instincts for possession, and urges for continuity. Not unexpectedly in the human animal these instincts become greatly sophisticated. We alone predict mortality. We value tradition. We intellectually appreciate creation as an act of election besides one of elemental drives, and we accept the responsibilities of that choice. This basis underpins the outsized psychological lever to human parenthood, the curiosity to give the experience a try, remembering meanwhile our own parents and our own childhood, measuring goals toward being parents ourselves, wishing selfishly to reap some maternal and paternal happiness from the process, even enjoying the genetic game of spotting in our kids Mom's cinnamon eyes or Dad's curls or Grandma's dimples and their carrying these family signatures forward while we aging folks edge toward the graveyard. And our children will always look at Mom and Dad and realize, "Those two **made** me."*

But, to my belief, the essence of parenthood is not the eyes nor the curls. It is not the ovum and the spermatozoon. Those tears at Mom's funeral, or Dad's, fall for other reasons.

Tears, and smiles, are not the coin or compensation for biological debts. Love of parent is not automatically a bill come due.

Authentic parenting is the intertwining of lives over that lengthy road from the blind dependence of infancy to old age. The bond between child and parent is the bond of repetition, of the same face and the same voice, day after day, decade after decade, with each experience, each life lesson, constructing what becomes unique and inimitable. This routine of connectedness is forged by the trivial and mundane as much as—if not more than—any momentous events of a life's span. You recognize parenthood when the same person fills up your breakfast cereal bowl on 3,000 different mornings, tries to teach you how to wink with either eye, fixes your broken shoelace, tickles to make you laugh at a lame joke, embarrasses you by hiding Easter eggs on the open lawn so that sweetheart you can find them (at ages four, five, even six), reminds you irritatingly every other day to brush your teeth, never forgets your favorite color is purple, instantly recognizes your voice on the telephone, gets emotional when you get emotional, plugs up your bloody nose with paper napkins after you take a high dive into the Turquoise River. Did I miss anything with this list? Everything.

*We feel sad when a parent dies because part of **us** is also lost—a material part, a factual death of our shared living. This explains the meaning of "Happy birthday to **us**" that begins with a birth.*

Now, back to the question once again, of whether government or ideology could ever successfully replace our traditional parenthood. Definitely a cultural system can become powerful enough to override natural parent-child bonds. In the highly developed Mayan-Aztec civilizations of Mesoamerica, among the thousands of ritual executions were many children, including children offered up as voluntary sacrifices. Other examples exist throughout history and therefore the question behind the question is: What sort of government, what sort of ideology, what sort of risk, when the culture is based primarily on instructed precepts and no longer anchored by the joint lives of a single family?

To date in our human history the scorecard for any attempted centralized control of culture (pejoratively termed "authoritarianism") has not produced happy results. Suppression and eventual repression of society has been almost the default method to keep a steady hand on the reins of power. What begins *as gentle persuasion—infused softly into religions, schools, media—becomes propaganda and ends, when it must, as legal dictate. The problem is a problem of structure and order of size. Amorphous "government" cannot understand or experience individuals. Government exists as its own organism, seeking its own survival as every organism does. But this organism is a **system**, a **machinery**, unembedded in much human context.*

The old troublesome dichotomy of scale returns. As our world, composed of discrete persons with their families, increases in number, the pressure for a compensating outside organization grows apace. And as the relationship between both sides becomes bulkier, the more diluted is their contact, leaving a weaker and weaker intensity, until government functions more and more with abstract categories instead of with the citizens. A rigid command government with its top-down command economy will want a similarly fixed society rather than a bottom-up culture, where the expressions of individuals filter up to influence or contest the leadership. But unknown is if we in fact require a degree of cultural "disorder," allowing enough mixed societal DNA for healthy evolutionary survival of our species. That is to say, to extend the Darwinian parallel, could an authoritarian government ever allow the change and adaptability necessary to confront an unpredictable future.

Aspirationally humanity might reinvent itself and construct a superior system of self-rule, meaning a more balanced one, meaning closer to not being "ruled" at all. Aspirationally—somehow short of raw indoctrination—society might evolve and naturally harmonize, agreeing on common values, accepting common limits of behavior, without homogenizing away individual rights and spirit.

That day of evolution has not arrived, nor does that day wait nearby off stage, as far as I can tell. It is potential only. But potential (as noted elsewhere) is a real thing. Or, in a more pessimistic mood, we could suppose that this dichotomy of ruler-and-the-ruled will always remain a dilemma, an unavoidable collision of principle. For to solve the dilemma a government would need to function, ironically, like that loyal parent, that same loyal face, who remembers your favorite color is purple.

For now, at least, no equal substitute for a mother and father exists, or to be accurate, for good mothers and fathers or good parenting. Not to be forgotten is how much effective parenting, like effective leadership in general, depends on an efficient distribution of labor—preferably, a sufficient division of actual deep commitment. Governments lack the structure ever to understand intimately or care for a billion individual citizens. Even parents will be challenged in properly loving their own children if beyond some functional number. Only a limited amount of hours and emotional energy can be divided among separate lives, despite the finest of motives.

While culture does influence parenting, the amassed network of personal parenting forms the basis of a newborn's foundational culture. Expressed more directly, in our lives today the family is the primary medium to instruct values. When the family proves sound their children have a strengthened path forward. The exhortation to "pull yourself up by your own bootstraps" may encourage or rescue a few struggling individuals. Best would be that the family and the culture together grab hold of everyone's bootstraps. I personally believe that the baby who is hugged has an honest chance for eventual success, regardless of the baby's circumstance, creed, or color. I believe that any child who learns and practices an expectation of achievement, whether modest or grand, will have an equal chance to attain it. All people respect confidence when they see its presence. All people respect self-respect.

Essay #15

Designing the Best Possible Government

Start with the best possible citizen.

[Explication: Finish with the same thing.]

Six

Here I am again speaking about parents. Or anyhow thinking of parents. Predictable of me?

Once upon a time (four days before my sixteenth birthday) we buried my mother. Always a slender woman, at the end I suspect she weighed less than one of those starved waifs we spot on street corners in film documentaries about terrible world wars. Like them her eyes had gotten too large for her face, which made her seem more a child, more youthful, illogically, since she was dying. I could shift her around in the bed with one arm.

Dying is a curious slow-motion event when it takes almost two years, and especially when it won't finish up properly. Observers might adjust to the whole downhill slide. What a big lie that would be.

The idea of how a mother can vanish right before your eyes is incomprehensible, reminding me more than anything of Dr. Bartleby's trickiest Final Questions, where no answer comes along to explain the impossible except the impossible itself. How does your mother move from the present tense to past tense, to a *was*, how change her from existence to "non-existence," an empty category suspiciously imitating Dr. Bartleby's fictional word *nothingness*. Death is such a complete thief. It gathers up what has been unique in all of time and extinguishes it for all of time. No wonder we collect and store the memories of the dead. A Beretta M9 may shoot a bullet and take away a life, but as Essay #4 says, "Nothing kills faster than forgetting kills."

Two years allow many opportunities for a child to hunch forward at the corner of a chair and watch its mother follow a discouraging routine. First would come those hopeful small spells of stable days and nights, moments of near normalcy, treasured moments we packed with the usual banter and family routine. Then would return those longer and longer periods— as predicted by our army of helpless doctors—of nasty decline. On one morning my mother might, at our front door, send me off to school with a squeeze on the shoulder and a bold wink, saying "Go get 'em, Sweetie." Follow this with a morning when she might not get out of bed. Follow this with two mornings of staying in bed. Follow this with a whole day of bed. Follow this with a morning, when somehow, there she stood in the kitchen making my breakfast.

"I can make my own breakfast," I told her, scolding her. She looked false to me, like a broken version of my mother, leaning against the counter, holding herself up with one hand, scooting a pan around with the other.

"You sound angry," said my mother.

Angry, I was. I was hating something. I was hating this false picture of my mother, hating that my real mother had already gone away.

"Now don't be mad." said my mother. "Nobody needs to be mad about anything. Even I'm not angry. See me smiling?" The mother was braver than her child, obviously, but how much wiser never became revealed to me, never until later when Dr. Bartleby shoved my nose back into my mother's blood-soaked pillow.

That morning, an ignorant child, I only repeated, "I can make breakfast."

"I know that you can, know it very well. Just let me do a few little things for you a few more times. Please?"

Forgive my childhood self, that my dying mother had to ask *please* to me, in order for her to help *me*, when the reverse should have been the case. As fate would prove, the reverse finally did become the case.

My father, my mother and I, we never prepared ourselves for the conclusion of our family story, assuming that there can be options to the inevitable. Yet my mother had her wishes and tried, on several short-circuited occasions, to speak on difficult topics. I still remember these episodes, unfortunately.

Right in the middle of an evening meal, tapping a fork against her plate to catch our attention, the plate holding a paltry half-slice of toast and a scoop of unseasoned cottage cheese, my mother announced—reminded us—that she wanted to be cremated "when she died."

My father acted offended. "Well, sure," he announced back. "Same for me when I die."

"Yes, but I want, I guess, to hear again that for certain my body won't be stuck in a box underground, with my body slowly coming apart. I despise that concept."

"Whoa!" exclaimed my father, turning to me, who sat there petrified now, awash with a new set of images. "You hear her? Boxes. Underground. Never! Nobody here will end up down there—my promise." He managed a believable guffaw. I credit him for that willpower.

My mother started to speak again, but when my father raised his eyebrows along with his hand, she decided against it, stopping. The discussion closed. And I was glad. Back to eating for us three, although like my mother not much food went into my mouth either.

Because she regularly refused the prescribed sedatives and pain medications, many grim days came for my mother, which we recognized without her expressing any complaint, other than those eyelids squeezed shut or sharp sucks of breathing. I would have preferred hearing a loud groan or raw curse, forcing me to share her suffering, and not joining my father to pretend our lives had stayed unchanged. On one of her dark days—a dark winter's night, literally—my mother gathered us in the living room for exactly the purpose of talking about our changed lives.

"My two darlings," she said, with a patient small smile, as sweet as a charming young girl might do, "I realize you both would be better off if I drugged myself asleep some days, like today in particular, when I'm pretty much a limp sack of potatoes that you need to haul around from room to room. Forgive me, you two? But you do know my stubborn personality by now, and you know how important it is to me that my mind keeps sharp to the very last."

My father challenged her instantly: What did Melody intend by "the very last"?

"When you two will be alone, without me."

"Alone?"

"Stewart, hear me out." My parents referring to each other by first name meant the mood in the air had everywhere tightened. "I want you both to accept without question that it's still me here, still me talking and thinking, regardless of how bad things look. However bad I *look,* it'll still be *me.*"

"Of course," said my father, pitching his tone to land, oddly, between impatience and reassurance. "Of course, of course. You are you. We believe that. Of course."

"Stewart. It's horrible enough turning into an invalid. Agreed. But becoming sort of a vacant mind, or getting dismissed, not to be your wife, and not a mother anymore, is unbearable for me. Stewart?"

"Easy there. Why get twisted up over nothing or next to nothing?" My father, needing to combine his final lines of defense, brought out his irresistible grin and his Marine method to victory: a direct assault against the insurmountable enemy. "Nobody here's going away. Nobody gives up. In time, we'll win. In time, you'll see."

Did my father, my savvy father, truly believe what he said? Probably. Belief is tethered to hope and survival and such.

I sat there next to them, desperate to trust him. My mother must have known different. Yet she smiled herself, not breaking apart my father's habits, protecting him in her own manner, while she still could, similar to her making a few more breakfasts for me.

In time, we'll win? Dr. Bartleby's Time had another plan.

Months came and went. My mother also did "go away," despite promises otherwise. And months after those months a police official telephoned our home to report that the Beretta M9 had been "released from the evidence locker" back to its owner. I was there when my father received the call.

Without hesitation my father responded, in a low voice, so low he apparently needed to repeat his words. "I'm saying, that I won't be reclaiming the gun. I'm asking, if you people there would dispose of it, however you choose." This was the last reference ever to our "family heirloom" as my father himself had once, fondly, identified the Beretta M9.

To tie up loose ends—two loose ends—my father and I soon discovered we had not only lost a wife and a mother, but the old intimate dynamic between us. Often we seemed strangers in a strange house, a lifetime away, for instance, from our Mason's Mill hours together. And we never closed the distance between us. My father tried his best, I suppose, but meanwhile he had lost both vitality and his famous smile. He wrote his confessional letter to me. He stuck to his job to earn money for my college. At that point he retired and waited impatiently to turn old, which happened, and during that wait I can't recall a single conversation when we looked each other in the eye.

What else to expect? Why accuse anyone or anything but me?

I was the family's traitor. Death's hand was mine, just as I admitted here to everyone at the beginning.

Essay #16

What to Do About Your Death Problem

Blame it on your parents.

[Explication: Remember who got you into this fix
in the first place.]

Essay #17

How Long Will Our Human Race Survive?

How lucky do you feel?

[Explication: In the end, not long enough.]

Seven

Dr. B:

I neglected writing you for a smidgen, according to my calendar, and more than a smidgen according to my guilty conscience. Truth is, and truth it shall be, I find myself slunk down deeper than customary into an overcast mood at the anniversary of my mother's death. These cloudy feelings drag me down and slow me down, including at work. But did I ignore your manuscript?

No!

Let me explain. Or attempt an explanation. A dozen years had passed since I last visited my mother's cemetery site, where a memorial plaque marks her cremated remains. Yet this week I returned again, and why? (Now my explanation tries to do its explaining.) What I can observe is that I carried your manuscript with me and those few pages inside a folder allowed me, and likely forced me, to visit once again. It embarrasses me to admit this behavior to you, the author, but presumably we're beyond embarrassment by now. Your pages stayed inside the folder. I had already done the reading beforehand, as you well suspect. That skinny (very skinny, dear author) folder itself apparently provided a thick enough shield for me.

With your folder firmly in one hand, the other hand shading away a late morning sun, I could now stand here, before my mother's remaining spot on earth, and what should I be feeling, or thinking? Dr. B, I had a dizzy sensation, a lack of focus, my every idea being bounced around, tumbled inside a vacuum, one idea upward, another idea downward.

To gain balance, and orderliness, I sat down on the fastidiously clipped lawn.

My disorientation came from the uncertainty of how to solve my mother's absence, how to categorize her disappearance, or if instead, being straightforward, I needed to completely erase her from this ongoing reality around me. Possibilities for rescuing her slipped into my mind, Dr. B, some self-mocking, some trivial. I could invent a religion where we automatically rendezvoused to hold an eternal chat. Or I could amend this bronze plaque here in front of me, that metal object presently summarizing my mother's life by an empty span between two numerical dates. Underneath those numbers I would order engraved:

Melody—

More Music Than Any Song

Or:

Melody—

The Name We Will Always Sing

Or: Any other lines of semi-poetry that—fingers crossed—will inform the world about my mother without sounding too silly.

But would my tiny public shout-out about this Melody person make any difference, Dr. B? Will the world care? Will it make my mother slightly, slightly tangible again? Honestly, no. Honestly, I think my real intent is patting myself on the head to soften my remorse. Visits to cemeteries are sometimes considered as unpleasant confrontations with your own mortality. But between you and me, my being alive frequently amounts to a lot of trouble, hardly worth the effort. When my mother became sick I wished hourly I could trade places with her, to let me be dying and her the healthy one—and this fantasy sticks with me today, absolutely a child's wish.

Dr. B, it angers me not to have another solution available. Seemingly my brain refuses to accept this magician's hocus-pocus disappearance of my mother, now-you-see-her, now-you-don't, altogether a sneaky trick of deception, right? Yet how does your Essay #2 explain mortality? It describes death with a totally blank page.

At the cemetery, sitting on the grass, the *Final Questions* manuscript pressing on my lap, certainly I hadn't forgotten your explanations (your reassurances, your admonitions?) that our caretaker memories of the dead are their final, and fragile, strands of existence. Yes. Fine. But I want my actual mother to hear me one more time, that part of her which always floated out from . . . from her "neural energy" (I believe you defined it) into thoughts and emotions. That same part of her, Dr. B, that I once recognized there in her face, and comprehended, without spoken words. I want my mother to connect back to me and know what I never had a chance say. What is not material is not combustible, correct? That "part" of my mother, the Melody part, must have survived the crematorium oven, correct? Where do I find this part now, Dr. B?

Tell me—as I believe you will—how I miss by a mile the

key about living and dying, and tell me I *did* have many chances when my mother understood me, and tell me that without doubt she already *knew* ahead whatever her child felt or might say. But Dr. B, how could I ever cry to her about the end before her end had happened?

Dr. B, after several revisits to Essay #16 and Essay #17 with your usual snappy answers, I suspect my personalized complaining here about death must have dragged on and on and into a burden for you. You seem impatient with the subject of death or flat out tired of it. Somebody's whining about dying? Again? Well then, stupid, scold your parents for your existence and your subsequent problem. Dr. B's intolerance makes sense. Besides, being ungrateful always looks petty.

So hurrah, to you my determined editor, and my comrade-in-arms, for here we still are, rolling along together, squeezing the juice out of thirty tissue-thin essays. I sincerely hope my few pages never prove a trial to you, either professionally or privately.

My sincerity with you, and concern, arise especially from

your potent remembrances of your mother, or more accurately, your painful disappointment that this remembering her is the paltry leftover of a valuable life. It follows that my essays on dying equally disappointed you. I can admit that they disappoint me as well. They rudely clang, flippant and dismissive, almost hostile about the subject. Safe to say, keep these essays far away from anyone's deathbed.

*Nevertheless, congratulations to you. With your editorial eye you detected and classified my genuine fatigue with this massive lump of a topic. Here all we humans eventually pause. There in front of us death looms, an enormous pile of evidence, and every single person sees it, watches it grow, knows that such massive lumps do not somehow get picked up or shoved aside. But despite having that knowledge each and every person is going to think and think and think about the big pile, wondering if it might, hopefully, be a mirage. **Our conclusion**: People choose to stay alive, typically. People prefer not to die, typically. Teach me something new! Not necessary to repeat this! And repeat it. And repeat.*

Death is inevitable enough to intermix it as a catalyst of time/process itself, gathered along with other near-synonyms and associated processes such as the overall sweeping categories we often term as elimination-destruction-dissolution-reconstitution.

Customary cliches about death being a requirement for life are not wrong. Each day a human body sloughs off billions of dead cells to allow new cells to live. Taking a larger view, as we are often reminded this same human body owes its factual existence to pieces from dead stars. Therefore everywhere in the universe we find dying partnered with living, destruction birthing creation, all informing us that our human fixation with mortality amounts to little more than a catch basin for self-pity.

With death this common, will it ever, rightfully, become simply . . . boring?

Not for us. For us, no other event so commonplace is so unique. While the universe ignores your mother's death, you refuse to follow along and instead do a turnabout, ignoring the universe. One cheer for our team.

Remember (again) our Essay #1 about "humanity," with the blissfully suicidal supernova and an insignificant flatworm that "tries to stay alive"? As a flatworm is a creature and a star can never be, we humans exceed the flatworm by as much. The worm reflexively twitches away from danger to survive. We humans, in comparison, can comprehend our individual stamp in time and space, forged by our actions and retained in our consciousness, realizing meanwhile that this precious entity (our being) is scheduled for complete vanishment. Subsequently, in protest, we create defiant religions and philosophies. We intend to beat back the darkness with the light of language. Another cheer for our team?

Because, by this dying, we conceptualize the totality of our loss, a crucial demonstration of how we can exceed the flatworm is by choosing this death, contrary to nature. This our colleague the worm would never do. There exist histories of humans electing to accelerate their own elimination, or risking their own end to serve an imagined higher cause— what we sometimes define as heroism. Undeniably this action confounds the mechanical universe. And another cheer for our team?

*Presumably the ultimate wish—yours, everyone's— is that we in some fashion defy the universe on and on, forever. Loving your mother as an example and we each want our participation at the time/process party never to stop. Could **homo sapiens** ever pull off such a stunt?*

Our chances for physical immortality we wrote about earlier, you and I. But a question this elemental deserves second and third thoughts even if only for the sport of it.

Begin with planet Earth, our homeland, because immortality is moot without a place to stay alive. Earth (currently) provides us with a (usually) habitable crust which wraps around an unstable ball of pressurized iron, the ball's center estimated to be as hot as the sun's surface. Accordingly the crust constantly wrinkles and erupts. The planet ball itself—flung through space—is open prey to speeding objects, with collision velocities high enough, violent enough, to obliterate civilizations. If our planet by mercy avoids all these localized threats, our sun will then do the destroying, when it expands to evaporate the seas and cook the land. In short, our earthly home, too, must die. While eons may appear to us as without an end, those eons shall pass, and our tiny blue ball must die.

Without an eternal Earth, how would **homo sapiens**, *our favorite species, achieve this "eternity" ambition? We will valiantly pretend the question is not pointless.*

—To review the basics: First, we assume that the human race has stabilized its environmental demands on our limited planet. We assume that universal energy and reliable nutritional needs have been met. I judge the probability of achieving these goals at 90%.

—Second, assume that human health and longevity have extended to secure levels without negative social consequences. I judge the probability of this at 75%.

—Third, assume that the human race has at

last organized itself politically, economically, culturally into a common block with unified social self-interests, also allowing individual creativity. Assume that wars become historical relics. I judge the probability of all this at 40%.

*—Fourth, assume that when the sun at last begins to misbehave, or when our Earth decides to freeze or sweat, **homo sapiens** nonetheless learns to adapt/adapt/adapt, evolve/evolve/evolve, and carries onward. I judge the probability of this at 30%.*

—Fifth, assume that when the Earth turns inhospitable, we humans conduct a space escape and leapfrog ourselves out of the dying solar system, finding another peaceful planet by another friendly star. Assume we transport along with us enough reproductive potential with enough technology to guarantee the survival of the species. I judge the probability of this mission at 0.0001%.

*—Finally: Assume that the above bundle of assumptions hits the jackpot of success against their absurd odds. Even then, even so, a neighboring galaxy already spins on its path to join our own Milky Way, aiming to upset the human apple cart. At some point—at some station along the time/process line, whether sooner or very much later—assume that a solemn group of **homo sapiens** will face each other, speaking a final*

Final Goodbye, feeling what you feel now when saying goodbye to your mother. Only for them, the future them, there will not be any mothers or fathers that follow. I judge the probability of this at 100%.

Now what? The inevitable extinction of our species—does such a guarantee, of such a mutual fate, diminish to any degree your single sadness over a single mother? Scarcely. Does predicting total loss of total humanity minimize the loss of the briefest individual life? Scarcely. Abstractions function nicely in the classroom, I heard my father state, but less well on the battlefield, or in the heart.

No wise rationale, no ingenious excuse, no tender sympathy, changes the finality of death. Let the tears flow if we wish. Tears honor the life lived, not its disappearance. Dying, we do realize, is universal, essential, acceptable as the essential must be accepted, yet we need not admire death. The most logically justified euthanasia remains a reluctant goodbye. A mercy killing—although not a misnomer—spells out at best an emotional contradiction. According to fundamental human nature, greetings of hello are happier than departing farewells. Therefore let human nature be.

Should you choose to grope deeper into the hereafter to

find your mother, deep into the fantastical and the wonderful, posit a claim that every human thought conceived on Earth, like photons of projected light, have all broadcast their energy beam out through the cosmos. And traveling at timeless speed along those eternal courses, there among the mixed babble of those voices, you and your mother might cross paths once again, and repeat your favorite words to each other. Or, more fantastical yet, away on a remote ersatz planet where demigod wannabes have turned quantum shenanigans into child's play, idle minds might reverse and reconstitute these earthly mental beams back into their flesh-and-blood human sources. (No, I refuse to judge the probability percentage of this happening. Who am I to calibrate acts of wonderment?)

Ultimately, my friend, I find the most practical summation of death is the same as of life, and offers us advice elsewhere frequently given. Life equals your turn but not your eternity. You get born already aboard this moving bus. Thank (or blame) a vast network of ancestors for the ride as you take in the view.

Eight

Dr. B:

My mother, my father, my tragedy, my guilt, my days, my nights, my no-exit journey alone aboard this bus ride you describe—I wanted Brown Eyes to join me for the trip. Companionship meant everything to me. It still does. I needed Brown Eyes and I wanted Brown Eyes to need me, a type of living equilibrium, or a mutual salvation to make it sound more religious. Otherwise traveling on my one-way bus is just a one-way conversation, talking to myself. I hate that idea! Already I'm tired of this unavoidable reflection there in my mirror and more than anything, please, I hoped to find an escape hatch out of my own consuming personhood, that "cage" you mention in Essay #18.

Essay #18

Men, Women, Whatever, Whyever

Selfhood is a cage with few exits.

[Explication: Go out, invite in.]

A shy admission, Dr. B: Your manuscript, having no Table of Contents, forced me to peek ahead in search of an essay titled "What Is Love?" or "How True Is True Love?" or "Love It or Leave It" or any reference whatsoever to romance. I had no luck finding one, not strictly. The closest piece is Essay #18, which upon reflection—and I gave it a lot—could be your eleven-word precis of a 500-page tome on love. You agree?

As you can tell, I dearly desire not to abandon my dreams about "love." I believe with all my "heart" that I "love" my Brown Eyes. (Past participle "had loved," I'm supposed to say.) But possibly you, Dr. B, believe that defining "love"—like any of those helpless abstractions you avoid, such as "The purpose of life" or "Why does existence exist"—only amounts to a quagmire of subjectivity, not worthy of an authoritative essay. If Dr. B did put together an essay on "What is love" or "How to find love" it could resemble this:

FINDING LOVE

Pick your favorite flavor of ice cream

and gobble it all up.

[Try not to get a tummy ache.]

Look there, Dr. B, I might learn the knack of writing tiny essays, your version anyway.

But, like a starving dog gnawing on its last bone, I can't let go of my hunger for another human soul to be my . . . my . . . my (my what?) . . . my life's mate—if anybody uses that word anymore. Or I can try an expression even more antiquated and out of mode, yet more rudimentary and the most simple: I want this other human to "be mine." No kidding, you heard right, the childishly possessive statement stamped on cheap Valentine candy hearts—"be mine"—this I want, and at my age. And if you ask me, Dr. B, what "be mine" means in specifics, I might churn out a million paragraphs, or draw a blank. I do know that "be mine" strikes the inner me as genuine. The inner me? Dr. B, you can decide whether this fuzzy description is intellectual cowardice.

To honor my own view of myself as rational and educated, supposedly I should challenge my emotional ambitions, should ask if I merely represent another hoodwinked sucker of Hollywood movies and prince-princess paperback stories. Am I, partly even, a dumb bit of flotsam, floated along by the tide of popular culture? (A respectable editor would delete this metaphorical overreach. Clearly here is one editor willing to lose respect for private gain.)

Believe it or not, in the office at work I dared to push poor Herbie about ever having been "in love." I did use a flimsy pretext where an author announces in her (rejected) manuscript to us that she had "fallen in love" with the excitement of topiary sculpture. "Would we blue-pencil out a sentence like that?" I asked Herbie, who lives with his sister, has for decades, both unmarried. Herbie didn't follow my question, he said, and I explained, "Can a person really *fall in love* with plants?" Herbie still didn't follow, he said, so I asked, "We need a definition of *love* here, don't you think?" Herbie, I could see, was turning into defensive stone. I said, "We'll approach this from another angle. Have you been in love, Herbie? Once?" Insult, horror, were the possible messages on Herbie's face, as if I'd asked him to strip off his clothes, including underwear. "Forget about it," I told him. "I *love* creative pruning myself, in fact."

Dr. B, I apologize again for any meanness to my colleague Herbie. I promise, no mischief was intended, and I only hoped to jolt an innocent man into an innocent response—truth from the mouths of babes kind of idea. My excuse is to blame my desperation.

How desperate? Well then, if this "love" doesn't already exist, I'll invent love on my own, thank you very much.

Will you accept the compliment, my friend, and value it, if I now select you as my exemplar of humanity instead of a flatworm? Worms notably set no requirements for love. I write you further tomorrow.

----

*Yes, double yes, the word **love** has ages ago been ruined by its scattered shotgun usage. Anytime, when we reach into our verbal weaponry for some emphasis, and anywhere, from the trivial to the legitimate to the "desperate"—to borrow your highest designation—we casually pull the trigger and fire off that lethal word. (Sing along: Any overblown metaphor you can do, I can do better . . . I can overblow any metaphor better than you.)*

*I suppose we forgive our abusing the word **love** because, happily, our demand for such a word must be great and varied. A few highlights:*

*—We can **love** ourselves. (Rhetorical use for "self-respect" and "self-preservation." If otherwise applied, is diagnosed as an unhealthy "narcissism.")*

*—We can **love** our nation. (Rhetorical use for "honor" and "cultural identification" and "tradition." Our personal life experiences become embedded in the language and history of our nationality.)*

*—We can **love** the human aggregate. (Rhetorical use for "altruism" and public "devotion to others." Saints are sometimes called "embodiments" of universalized love.)*

*—We can **love** a friend. (Rhetorical use for "platonic friendship.")*

*—We can **love** our family. (Literal use for highly focused levels of "commitment" and "attachment." Familial bonds are typically both instinctual and created.)*

*—We can **love** another lover. (Literal use for itself, "love," when the word is utilized by you, my ambitious friend, and by most earnest others in the modern age. And fair enough, do consider Essay #18 for starters.)*

What if we speculate whether "love" was present in prehistory, as far back as the cold caves or desert shelters of nomadic hunters, when staying alive for many of them amounted to a handful of years. Did these people have any space in their brief and dangerous lives for "love"? Under enchanting starlight, did face bend over face and someone say the equivalent of "I love you"? Could it be, that "love" is too abstract when the belly is too empty? Could it be, that leisure and language have to expand before the word "love" becomes desired, conceived, invented, used?

Lastly, might personalized "love," as you mean it and want it my friend, revere it, your Brown Eyes love, be a singular bump along an evolving emotional path for humankind? All bumps have a Before and an After.

We continue speculating on our cave ancestors, there under their moonlit skies, and wonder if they ever embraced and had Hollywood romance—no, had genuine romance, genuine devoted love, as we insist to define it. Well, to speculate is to speculate. Granted, our ancestors mated, a biological imperative that fosters a possessive bond and a joint responsibility. On this elemental level even a few animal species form pairs, for a generational cycle at least, occasionally much longer. Also we know that early humans organized into tribal groups, the better to provide shared protection and a more consistent supply of food and, through sexual proximity, more reliably to propagate their continued existence. Breeding may well have begun as a communal action—essentially random—before morphing into established forms of polygamy, whereby a dominant partner (normally male) reserves the general rights to any mating partners. This arrangement follows the rule found elsewhere in the animal kingdom, of supporting the genetic stream from the most successful candidates. Extended into contemporary times there remain limited areas in our world where the practice of multi-partner marriages still exist due to cultural, economic, or legal motives.

But throughout today's world at large, apparently after developing from modern westernized thought, the idea of "love" as its own central goal in life has taken hold. You and I, being students of history, can skip retracing and repeating the specific developments in social and intellectual events that narrowed focus from group loyalties down to institutional obedience down to individual worth. We might express it as a growing trust in personal responsibility and a growing belief in our personal value. And therefore to whatever, or to whomever, carries such a high value we can dependably give "love."

Does love have a future? In the long haul, we humans could move beyond our biology, could construct ourselves to live contentedly without any emotional dimension, be programmed to find happiness outside of the self or body, as some classic Thinkers proposed in theory, and as some religious ascetics today attempt. With the aid of science and ideology and the forces of survival we could imagine your Brown Eyes category of love in decline, becoming a quaint anachronism found among a few backward sects.

Yet, once more, what does our definition of "love" represent, for the two of us writing here: the opposite of "aloneness" or "isolation." The religious devotee hopes to be wed to an otherworldly perfection. The philosopher abstractionalist does the same, codifying an intellectual hierarchy of ideals. Both avoid the flawed and mortal human creature as being too transient and inappropriate for the purest respect and devotion. However, you and I, my friend, maintain or wish the opposite, that exactly this, our imperfection and mortality, make the giving and receiving of full commitment the most ambitious "love," while the most needed.

And as an overarching government can never duplicate a successful family, in turn the family cannot imitate the dynamics of a successful couple. View this conclusion as the result of a reduced number (2), conjoined inside restricted time and space (a lifetime), forming a veritable twinness through sharing. Should the concept or practice of "loving" ever alter into something less personally human, we present romantics would rate life poorer with that loss. Possibly today we find ourselves participants in the last Golden Age of Love.

Overall I have a hunch, just a hunch, that "love" did not originate from an aspirational experiment worked out in the modern age by restless minds. The impulses seem too fundamental. Back in the unknown mists of our human story love must have lurked among those boulders, back when our ancestors presumably still impulsively copulated with the handiest tribal body, back long before "love" became a word. Somewhere, sometime back then, eyes met, eyes locked. Those eyes, speaking a soundless and inchoate language, said "You," "Me," "Us only." That moment—confusing even to them—may have been crushed by external realities. But we, my friend, would have recognized the look, easily translating those eyes.

Just a hunch.

Nine

Dr. B:

A hunch, did you say, Dr. B? Don't torment me with such luring dismissive understatements. A timeless, magical glance exchanged down by the stream, by the boulders? Those eyes! Dr. B, you're breaking my miserable heart. I once participated with such glances.

I bump against sleep some nights—most nights—awake, afraid I could die before I find a proper end for myself. Identify this proper end as the usual "happiness," or at a minimum, a sensible tidying up of life, the kind of final chapter we want to edit for a decent book, where the theme or plot gets organized and summarized into a satisfying conclusion. Is that a fair wish or a juvenile hope?

Reading your Essay #19 about happiness reminded me of my father's little homily about rainbows. I call it a little homily because I was little when he told it, and he used little words. Those little words made a big impression on the little me. During one of those family vacation outings I described earlier, somewhere under the open skies of western America, we drove into a mix of storm and sun with a gigantic rainbow. At this spectacle my father then concocted his tale, about a child "precisely my age," who spotting a rainbow "precisely like this one above us now," had packed a lunch "almost exactly like the boxed lunch on our backseat" and hiked off to discover the rainbow's end and the pot of gold waiting there, as promised by many legends. This child, reportedly, trudged along for many hours. "Now, did the kid finally find the end of the rainbow?" asked my father. "Yes?" I answered, clueless of any science but definitely locating a rainbow touching down off in the distance. "No," said my father, the geologist, "no, no. The rainbow moves away as you move ahead. Your eyes shift along with it until the rainbow disappears. You can never touch a rainbow. Are you disappointed? Do you think the child cried and didn't eat the lunch?" "Probably," I said, since that seemed reasonable to this little me. My father asked, "Was it wrong for the child to be disappointed?" "Maybe?" I said, hedging my bets on that suspiciously tipped question with a return question. My father had arrived at his message. This unhappy child, he explained, had already found the gold without noticing the evidence in plain sight. "Look up into the sky, see, see, a real treasure without having to move a single inch."

And then my mother had popped into the conversation and asked what if a person did hike over to where the rainbow seems to hit the earth, what would that person find? "Mud, most likely," said my father, "from the rain."

Essay #19

The 4 Basic Steps
to Find Happiness

One, two, three, four, repeat.

[Explication: An ambitious journey is its own destination.]

But, Dr. B, I can't replicate that child in the car. Rainbows and cheery homilies don't work for me anymore. I ruined rainbows, all by myself, doing serious wrongs I could never bear to tell you about. Besides this breast-beating, hair-pulling that I do a bunch—accept more of my apologies—directionless is what I am, lacking your Essay #19 happiness steps to follow, not even the first step, let alone numbers two, three, or four. What particular steps, I must ask, and what journey to whereabouts is ambitious enough, I must also ask. Ask, ask. If I could be more insightful, or more inventive, or had more grit, and could answer those questions on my own, then I would stop with the apologies. (And mark that last sentence as another complaint and another apology!)

Happiness. The ethical sinkhole of defining "happiness" is to fall into the abyss of equivalency. Think about it. One person's satisfaction might mean the same result as another person's regret. Or the pleasure from giving mercy might be no greater than the pleasure from taking revenge. Or my happiness might rank as more valuable than your happiness, should they come in conflict.

The safety net placed over this moral sinkhole constructs itself from a set of behavioral standards everyone together presumably accepts—judgments on what constitutes Good vs. Bad, Right vs. Wrong. These abstract rules, collected by common consent, have their own complicated history, and form the topic of the upcoming Essay #20. Putting these legal and societal rules aside for now, what does guide us, my friend, in the Wild West search for happiness, as we seek it here, there, anywhere? Is finding happiness just the process of wandering about lost without any map?

*Fortunately, no, we are not lost, not really directionless (to use your word), since you already **are** the map—you yourself— that particular map we draw as we develop, as individuals, from inside our cultures. My personal map is not your map, although overlaps may exist. Only you understand your own happiness. Only you understand your own ambition. Forget asking anyone else for such a map, including me. Never cheat yourself by escaping outside into a formulaic creed or doctrine in order to replace your map unless they are congruent by chance or choice. Only through deception can we pretend to substitute or abdicate our own happiness.*

I would repeat another primary point, if you grant me your patience for one more amateurish analogy. "Happiness" in my view, or according to my map, is not a state arrived at as a distant end goal, waiting for me, beckoning. Happiness is not some achieved culmination, reached by finally earning redemption at the gates of some salvation or other. Instead . . . here we use my analogy, and compare happiness to picking the ripest berries along a footpath. First you choose the best path where your best happiness berries grow. Next you keep an eye out for the plumpest berries with the richest color. You walk, you pick, you eat, you learn more about berries. Now and again a berry turns out more sour than sweet but you keep walking, keep looking, keep picking, keep eating. 1, 2, 3, 4. These must be the steps repeated in Essay #19? To conclude the analogy: After all, we eat (berries) not to starve. Happiness fills the stomach best.

I try to tone down or shy away from claiming any "happiness" that could, in probable fact, result from rationalization/accommodation/fatalism/relativism, such as by convincing myself that a tart berry is at least better than no berry, or that a tart berry at least would have been sweet next month, or that a pomegranate if not really a berry at least weighs more than a berry does. You get the picture. Plenty of "at least" excuses. I prefer taking a few extra steps down the path and picking a few other promising berries. And now, forthwith, I vow, I actually will conclude my analogy conclusion.

Preaching the tenets of "happiness" makes the speaker—this speaker—appear no different from a slick hustler at a homemade pulpit, a huckster, and I hate hearing it, doing it. "Behave like this! Believe that! 1,2,3,4!" Oh, I feel the sham of giving this advice. Yet you ask and I answer because we moved beyond dispassionate explication of a manuscript titled **Final Questions***. I answer only because I know more about you than you will ever dream.*

My most serious advice about happiness, my friend, is advice about **unhappiness***, which is the one condition we can truly control. I believe we purposely elect unhappiness as a method to punish ourselves for perceived failures or faults. Ludicrous as it sounds, we utilize unhappiness as a penalty for not being happy. Unravel that thought, my good friend. Untangle your own life. While unhappiness, in moderation, could arguably be a beneficial motivator, nevertheless we humans without hesitation can be unbelievably cruel to our own selves, not only to others.*

Ten

At this moment in my crescendoing experience with Dr. Bartleby, on the day when Dr. Bartleby wrote, almost accidentally, about knowing me more "than you will ever dream," I sat myself down and realized that next to nothing was an accident with Dr. Bartleby, whoever Dr. Bartleby was. This episode with its uneasy rush also showed me my vulnerability. I had, step-by-step, been opening my life wider-wider-wider to a stranger, a Dr. B. Bartleby, whose "B" could belong to either a man or a woman, just as my own given name isn't at all a gender reveal, an ambiguity which I sneakily exploit sometimes in written correspondence.

So thorough then was our ignorance about each other— our unspecified sex, one person acting like a pomegranate farmer, one person pretending to be an editor. Yet the farmer claimed somehow to understand the editor more "than you will ever dream."

And I believed this Dr. B. Bartleby. In my bones I believed, must have begun believing back when I first slit open that unimposing manuscript mailer on my desk, reading the paltry scant pages that were too outrageous to be nonsense. Whatever my belief, it tugged at me, kept *Final Questions* in my life, took away the many practical reasons to send the book back. Yes, I could see how I wanted to believe, desperately I suppose, but the voice—Dr. Bartleby's voice—constantly proved its legitimate power, its reality, with its attendant honesty.

I concluded that the fake editor should always listen to Dr. B. Bartleby. What I heard might surpass my dreams, as the pomegranate farmer for some reason had said.

Essay #20

What Is Goodness and What Is Badness?

The question's also the answer.

[Explication: To ask the question is the good.
Not to ask the question is the bad.]

Dr. B:

I think hard about your Essay #20, Dr. B.

It's no exaggeration to say I already thought about Essay #20 before Essay #20 existed, since back when I was (almost) age sixteen.

This week Essay #20 made me torture officemate Herbert again, when without provocation I asked him about his sister Naomi, the older sister he lives with, and his only surviving family member. I hardly believed the words coming from my mouth.

"There's a potential for evilness around us, waiting to happen," I said to Herbie, stopping unexplainably by his desk, a packet of manuscript pages in my hand. This particular manuscript had nothing to do with evil, and everything to do with pumpkins and gourds. "Do you agree, Herbie?"

Herbie eyed the pages held in my hand. He sat up straight in his chair—alarmed, or ready to be alarmed.

"I mean, Herbie, we see good and bad behavior in the world, existing side-by-side. You agree?"

Herbie (blinking rapidly) may have nodded.

"I mean, Herbie, anybody can commit one of these bad things, very bad things, including us, you and I can, correct?"

"Bad things?"

"Very bad things."

"Very bad things?"

"Very bad. What if Naomi were killed. Very bad."

A pale expression equaling "very bad" changed Herbie's already pale face. He said, "A speeding red semi-truck missed us by less than a yard once."

"And imagine if somebody *murdered* Naomi. How evil would that be, I wonder. How bad. Tell me."

"Tell you?"

"Tell me. How bad. Very bad?"

"Very, very bad."

"And imagine if *I* murdered Naomi, what would you think about me?"

"Pardon?"

"If I took away Naomi's life, what should happen to *my* life, would you say? Let's make it a legal judgment, if you don't mind, Herbie. For fun."

Being a sensible guy, Herbie found no fun potential whatsoever in our talk, and he turned his back on me, returning to his work as if never interrupted. A chance is, he turned his back on me forever, although later that day I observed him in animated conversation with our head editor Franklin, where I might have been their topic.

Will I be fired from my job here in this cozy publishing playhouse of gardens and kitchens? *Should* I be fired, Dr. B, for being a slackard? All my earnest hours I spend on only one book, your *Final Questions*. Using some unknown deception I still, in my mind, call myself your editor. Can you believe it? Your editor!

Or do I, underneath, Dr. B, want and hope to get myself removed?

Cancel that question. It converts you into becoming *my* editor. I'll answer the question on my own for once. Yes, I deserve to lose my position, deserve to be punished—that same severe self-punishment you earlier cautioned against in happiness/unhappiness. But Dr. B, intentional unhappiness, destructive unhappiness, can be totally justifiable.

Putting it bluntly, a bigger question or my own Final Question, is whether I am, in life's conclusion, a faulty person, a bad person. That biggest question I can, again, also answer myself—unlike most people—except I won't answer here in public from the shame, or from fright, from hurt, or add those together. *However* my silence never represents my denial.

I keep reading Essay #20, trying to fit myself into its logic, keep trying to find in Essay #20 a personal escape, a different answer to this biggest question other than my own answer, the answer only I can already know is true. Not even you, dear Dr. B, wise you with your final questions, will ever imagine the events behind my truth.

Right and Wrong. Good and Bad. Moral and Immoral. Virtue and Evil. Hero and Villain. We could go on, pairing other ethical opposites, other alleged antonyms.

Complexities and contradictions soon abound when probing into these abstract judgments, amused philosophers and artists for centuries having played havoc with notions of "good" and "bad" human action.

—All war is "wrong," yet individual wars can be "good," usually as determined and interpreted by the winner, thereby making war good and bad simultaneously.

—All behavior among animals is universally acceptable because "natural," while the identical "bestial behavior" by humans can be judged "unnatural," or "bad."

—Therefore while natural laws exist that govern survival, no such laws determine moral behavior, rather only adopted social codes that can vary between cultures.

Stop! Enough with stirring up the turbulent waters of ethical subtleties. My professor father made a decent income doing that intellectual stirring and never did touch base at the one sensible conclusion, which is Essay #20. Our world need never fear a person who travels life filled with an active moral self-suspicion. This sort of healthy doubt cuts across multiple societies with their admixture of lessons, commandments, rules, laws. My friend, do consider how no true villain will ever be heard uttering a syllable of private regret. Total evilness equates with total indifference.

*Back again to our childishly modest Essay #20. If you, my friend, decide to ignore it, to ignore this Essay #20, you also refuse to believe **Final Questions** entirely. Fine. This leaves me with my last method to gain your confidence, and your trust, by telling the story of XYZ, a story that along its way may demonstrate how completely I do understand you, my friend, as I alluded to once before—in a nearly reluctant sentence.*

But what would be the use of my XYZ story if beforehand you had dismissed it as false?

Dr. B, please, tell me the story.

Then: the story of XYZ, the story of a girl or boy, a man or woman, I do know which but elect not to specify, qualifying it as anyone's story.

Before XYZ there had been a sibling baby, who died at precisely age one month, exact to the day, an invisible sibling until XYZ was told on an eighth birthday, and was startled by the abrupt appearance of an unknown baby's photo album, a partial album with an unsmiling infant's handful of pictures inside. From that birthday onward—already when blowing out the eight candles (unsuccessfully)—XYZ understood the precious value of being a living child in this family and XYZ now understood how families altogether needed to be guarded and protected.

By XYZ's tenth birthday the father had lost a fingertip in a lawnmower accident, causing XYZ a week's worth of moody sniffling, despite parental jokes about the father "not being able to pick his nose anymore."

By (almost) XYZ's fourteenth birthday the father had taken XYZ on a road trip for a sentimental visit to the father's boyhood lands, where he told a hopeful lie about the mother's health. XYZ halfway still believed hopeful lies and fathers.

*By XYZ's fifteenth birthday the mother had translated the concocted Latin of her medical condition to XYZ, a progressive disease that no **cogito** could ever explain away into remission. XYZ began the first of many raggedy sleepless nights.*

Before (very much before) XYZ's sixteenth birthday the whispering had started. Even with the father out of the house, away at work, the mother always lowered her voice when asking about a pistol up in the bedroom closet. For purposes that seemed unclear, yet ever unpleasant, XYZ answered back in a matching whisper. Their whispered words began more and more to be a nauseous sound slithering across XYZ's stomach.

"Sweetheart, tell me again what kind of gun?"

"Well, a Beretta M9, Mom."

"You can reach it. Can get it down from the shelf. You have before."

"Yes, Mom."

"You know I couldn't bring the thing down myself. You know I'm stuck, mostly stuck, here in this bed. You know that."

"I know, Mom."

Days passed.

"Sweetheart, show the pistol to me."

"You don't like guns, Mom."

"Show me the thing, please. Show me you can bring the thing down."

Days passed.

"You can show me the pistol, Sweetheart."

"Once, Mom."

Days passed.

"Load the magazine. Isn't that how you say it?"

"Too dangerous, Mom, in the house."

"You know how."

"I know how."

Days passed.

"Too dangerous, Mom."

Weeks passed. Bullet shells have a nice metal slickness when rolled between the fingers. They give a satisfying **click** *when pressed into the magazine clip of a Beretta M9, each click really announcing **we mean business**. A faint metallic scent, blended with an oily sweetness, touches the air.*

Weeks passed. It requires a bit of strength to rack the slide back of a Beretta M9, loading the gun to fire.

"Way too dangerous, Mom."

"Show me."

"Way, way too dangerous in the house."

How many days passed? Many. Many more days passed, many more whispers. On one of those days the mother tells XYZ, "Tomorrow you can leave the thing in my nightstand drawer."

"No, Mom. No, no, no."

"You can. Why carry it from the closet each time?"

"No, no, no, no. Remember the safety rules."

"You can do it."

"Mom."

"Yes, you can."

"Mom."

The mother never explains. The mother never argues, never raises her voice. She is forever gentle, in her best motherly way. And she never uses the unfair lever of speaking aloud "if you loved me."

By XYZ's sixteenth birthday, or practically so, being nine days ahead, the mother stops XYZ, leaving for school. She sits at the edge of the bed, a pert smile on her face, her hair lately washed, tidy, lustrous, the hairbrush still in her hand. She makes a sweeping farewell gesture with the brush.

She calls, "I wanted you to see me smiling when we said goodbye this morning. Take a very good look, please, Sweetheart. See me?"

"I see you, Mom," says XYZ.

"You could smile back?"

No smile back. No wave back. No goodbye. XYZ refuses all symbols of separation.

When XYZ returns home from school, opening the front door, marching directly inside like a stout soldier, what does XYZ find? Nothing of surprise, to be candid.

The Beretta M9 lies flat and a contrasting dark on the milky white bedroom carpet. A starburst pattern of the mother's blood decorates a lace-trimmed pillowcase, and to make the picture somehow more histrionic XYZ recalls that this same pillow slip came from the mother's own mother. None of this cruel scene causes XYZ to cry. XYZ is too sick in the soul to cry. XYZ overall is sick of XYZ. XYZ has been sick of XYZ for a month, when XYZ first felt the choking power of a decision taking control. On her deathbed, the mother appears beautiful and grotesque, familiar and unfamiliar. XYZ watches her, a long and slow watching, in no hurry to phone the father or any authorities. XYZ is occupied, busy being sick of XYZ. XYZ will stay busy for years to come.

And that, my friend, is the story of this XYZ person, someone who remained stuck, too young to grow old.

Dr. B, I'm screaming to the heavens! Screaming! Dr. B, this XYZ story is *impossible* for you to tell, impossible, scaring me as scared as scary can be. Who is this Dr. B. Bartleby? Granted, you're the supreme master of connecting dots, but where did you find these dots to connect? Not from me. Or then who am I? Are you going to pretend that crazy me wrote your *Final Questions* myself, in order secretly to edit my own book and my own messy life? Don't pull that old trick on me, Dr. Bartleby. What's happening here? What?

You decide what the "happening here" is. You decide who wrote this book, or whether that matters.

But first let me complete XYZ's story, because it did not finish there in that bedroom with a gun on a white carpet.

A mother asks her young child to make an invincible mark on the eternal cosmos, changing the destiny of the world, reversing the supposedly inviolate rules of behavior. The child allows the impossible: love of mother replaces love of mother. This incalculable choice, this emotional equation, could never function in mathematics. This choice, this elective reaction, could never take place in physics.

As much as XYZ suffers, as much XYZ is heroic.

I have yammered constantly, my friend: The universe is an expanse of pure ignorance, its existence literally meaningless without the pinpricks of intelligence poking here-and-there, barely anywhere, in its unfathomable sprawl. Choice will never be discovered as an element anywhere in the outside cosmos, only in our elusive consciousness. The mother and XYZ again prove that free will is necessary even if by choosing that free will is not free.

But XYZ does not perceive the heroism. Not yet.

Later in life, at a humble grocery store, in its vegetable section, at a display of carrot bunches on sale—not asparagus— XYZ finds happiness. XYZ links up with Brown Eyes Somebody and finds a happiness so significant, so desired, that eliminating this same happiness at long last equals a proportionate fate for having loaded bullets into a Beretta M9. Using the many infinitesimal tricks that people invent to turn happiness sterile, XYZ pushes Brown Eyes far away. Applying a perverse calculation this sacrifice, too, is heroically brave, although unnecessary, although mistaken.

Will XYZ ever accept that sometimes heroism can hurt? Will XYZ ever accept XYZ's singular universe, a private one more complex than the sum of all those stars up in the sky?

Make a guess, my friend. You tell me.

Eleven

TO:

Dear Dr. Bartleby:

Last night I may have slept, but awoke too early, with my room, and the world, still black. For two lengthy hours I lay in bed watching night turn into dawn, thinking. I knew that this day would be the day I had to write you a final message. (That word "final" also rises up again.) This dawn, like all dawns, did arrive with its predictable regularity, and now I can't avoid the likewise predictable consequences of my own responsibilities.

It became apparent that your Essay #20 is the last one of the thirty in the manuscript I needed in order to reach my editorial decision. Essay #20—and your "XYZ" amplification of it—explain in totality what any reader might need in order to keep any intellectual (or emotional) feet solidly on the ground.

Due to all the artful profundity on display in the book, and in particular due to your willingness, tirelessly, to respond immediately to questions, I especially regret to report that we cannot publish *Final Questions*. The reluctant determination here by our staff was that your fine book does not fit into our specialized sales market, nor could be revised to do so.

Again, let me underscore how sorry I am to send such negative news. My apologies.

My dear Dr. B:

My friend, I won't send you some official dolt-headed rejection notice without following up with a corrective antidote of unadulterated honesty. *Final Questions* amounts to a brief high flight through the realms of science and philosophy and should "fit in" everywhere on this planet, no excuses! I, myself, went along on that flight, thanks to you, Dr. B, and I might be able to sell that experience, its obvious exhilaration, to my colleagues. I had hoped.

I imagined myself standing at the desk of chief editor Franklin McDermott, looking intently into his always friendly face, your little manuscript hidden behind my back, asking him, "Franklin, would we ever take a chance, ever risk publishing a kind of insane book, but an important book, one that wanders about 10,000 miles away from our usual food or flowers?"

I imagined Franklin smiling sympathetically. He usually does, bless him. I imagined Franklin asking me, "What do we know about this author?" A standard question among editors.

What do I know about you, Dr. B. Bartleby? Not much, right? Not your full name. Not how you—in complete contrast— know the unknowable, the impossible, about perfect strangers, and from afar, wherever that far place is located. When I went to return your manuscript today, I discovered no return address, discovered also that the stamps on your envelope packet had no postal cancellation. Mysteries left and right! And how can I return your manuscript without your address?

Now for my honesty part. While, true, I did imagine myself approaching kindly Franklin, that didn't happen. No one else here has ever heard about your manuscript. I kept *Final Questions* to myself, for myself, for strictly selfish reasons. From the start I realized we would never publish your book. In case you might wonder about it—oh yes, I'm humiliated, actually ashamed, to admit deceiving you, but also admit I'd repeat every minute of every deception in order not to lose the talking we had together. I considered us that way, "talking together."

Speaking of wondering, and honesty, I wonder if you found any motive to deceive *me*, with your considerable inventive wiles. Did you, in fact, have a philosopher father? Is the whole pomegranate milieu a humorous facade? Conceivably those homey details were designed to humanize you, and relax me, comforting me, each of which came to pass.

So, for a certainty, what do I know about you, Dr. B?

I know, for a certainty, only the important point—how much you're my friend. Which explains what? Which explains I want to reach back to the list (a hierarchy?) of love definitions that you once enumerated, and give two or three or four of these loves straight to you. Please accept them from me.

Have I embarrassed anybody with this blurting out of affection? Not me, Dr. B, not me. You'll catch not the faintest blush from me, for sure.

----

*Proudly I accept your valuable gift, my friend, or priceless gift I should clarify. In return I gift you **Final Questions** to keep, without mailing the manuscript back. Your gift is greater than* *mine, yet I do hope that **Final Questions** finds a welcome spot in some lower desk drawer of yours, where on special occasions it can be dusted off for the sake of positive memories.*

*And never concern yourself about not publishing my book. It will likely prove to be that all the big Thinkers presently in the world, and definitely the little Thinkers, such as any pomegranate growers, are clumsily wrong. But only a blind klutz would send **Final Questions** to a publisher whose #2 most popular book carries the title **Stews of Yesterday for Today.** I guarantee, this pomegranate farmer is not blind. On the other hand, or on the only hand, this particular farmer supposes that for any writer to become successful just requires pairing with one successful reader, whether brought into combination by luck, or by careful strategy. We make up that fortunate pair, my friend.*

Onward we sail, today, aboard our lovely middling planet, squinting at our sunshine star during the days, gawking at the sparkling eternity of the nighttime sky, often overwhelmed by the vastness of the unknown and the frailty of ourselves. However. Let us repeat endlessly, and not forget, about our own greater vastness, our own greater originality, and our exquisite awareness of mortality. For one last time, to return far rearward to Essay #1—paraphrasing it—we observe how a star or a galaxy may appear spectacular, as beautiful as any human abstract art.

Yet what alone discovers and determines and creates the beauty of both? Thinking makes importance.

*And by "thinking," remember always, I mean **thought**, not the physical mind, that apparatus with its mechanical energy. While every particle of matter, whether the tiniest or joined into an aggregate, elicits a vibrating force field, a **thought** remains a constant beyond measurement. Because of this the laboratory or psychological search to locate the whereabouts of **thought** remains useless. The presence of thought, from consciousness, demonstrates its reality by controlling our very actions.*

Solving a puzzle is always more entertaining than getting handed its answer. Accordingly, our fine Thinkers will carry on and on, building elaborate exploratory machines, filling pages with many elaborate speculations—scientific, mathematical, philosophical—producing terminology bursting in the air like exciting fireworks, some glowing brighter than others, some fading faster: multiverses, wormholes, mouseholes, negative mass, anti-gravity, dark energy, quantum uncertainty, observational inebriation, Big Bang, Little Bangs, No Bang—let me grab a breath before I continue. No, let me stop instead. You already heard the drill. First our school textbooks will state the facts or our gospel, then along will come heretical disagreement, then the heretical becomes the gospel, then comes the heretical again, then the gospel again.

*Possibly, probably, inching ahead, what had appeared increasingly complex turns out increasingly uncomplicated. As we probe the farthermost into the cosmos around us and into the cosmos within us, would it be so strange to discover that each ultimate challenge of describing our reality had the simplest solution? Down to whatever physical bottom point of analysis our world reduces itself, that informative endpoint then becomes a conclusion now obvious to us. The puzzle pieces fit together, even if shifting. The fun diminishes. **Whatever** is out there already waits, already **exists,** fixed, a period to a sentence.*

Here is what I want you to believe. Every Final Question that we can conceive, every mystery that we try to unwrap with chalkboards and computers, is not as sublime, or significant, or irreducible, as you and your mother. Of that Final Answer I am convinced.

Twelve

We'll consider this our goodbye, the Final Chapter for all our Final Questions. Dr. Bartleby's logic informs us that there can be no actual finality to finality, but please adapt my meaning. My meaning is that *Final Questions* rests safely away in a nearby drawer, as was suggested.

Last night I looked at the wide starry sky and shrugged my shoulders.

Last night I slept without any interruption from any dream. I almost miss them.

Lately, in the editorial Forward to a book we intend publishing here, called *Fruits for the Adventurous*, I personally composed a bouncy octave on pomegranates, using a Valentine motif for the color imagery. I titled the poem "Punica granatum," wanting to use a breathful of Latin, to maintain a family tradition.

I believe co-editor Herbert approves of my poem. He slipped me a mild smile, Herbie-sized.

www.ingramcontent.com/pod-product-compliance
Lightning Source LLC
Chambersburg PA
CBHW032302310726
48973CB00008B/2497